CANYON OF THE GUN

T. V. Olsen

Chivers Press • G.K. Hall & Co.
Bath, England Thorndike, Maine USA

This Large Print edition is published by Chivers Press, England, and by G.K. Hall & Co., USA.

Published in 2000 in the U.K. by arrangement with Golden West Literary Agency.

Published in 2000 in the U.S. by arrangement with Golden West Literary Agency.

U.K. Hardcover   ISBN 0-7540-3945-5   (Chivers Large Print)
U.S. Softcover   ISBN 0-7838-8733-7   (Nightingale Series Edition)

The text of this Large Print edition is unabridged.
Other aspects of the book may vary from the original edition.

Set in 16 pt. New Times Roman.

Printed in Great Britain on acid-free paper.

British Library Cataloguing in Publication Data available

Library of Congress Cataloging-in-Publication Data

Olsen, Theodore V.
    Canyon of the gun / T.V. Olsen.
        p.   cm.
    ISBN 0-7838-8733-7 (lg. print : sc : alk. paper)
    1. Large type books.   I. Title.
    [PS3565.L8C36 2000]
    813'.54—dc21   99–39439

CHAPTER ONE

Calem's fingers curved around the gunbutt with the easy reflex of practice, and the interval between his full-cocking the hammer and the whisper of steel clearing the waistband of his jeans was almost imperceptible. He aimed by instinct, bringing the old gun level, and then rammed it back into his waistband. He thought then, grinning a little, *That was good. Wonder what Jesse would say?*

His face sobered, and he raised a hand to his shirt pocket and dug out a few precious cartridges. He juggled them in his palm, thinking, *They should be gone all day. Why not?* Again he lifted out the gun, thumbed three of the shells into the well-oiled cylinder, and set the firing pin over the first. Holstering the heavy weapon, he turned and walked off a few steps.

At nineteen Calem had his full growth, a gaunt six feet three of it. He had shot up like wild willow in the last few years, and his big-boned frame already hinted at the beef to come. His chest and shoulders boasted more heft than his father's, and he could heave a fifty-pound feedsack into a loft six feet over his head and hardly know the effort. He had outgrown about all his clothes; turning now, he shifted his shoulders against his rough homespun shirt with a vague discomfort, but carefully, because sewing up the occasional torn seams of his exertions made an extra chore for Ma.

He eyed his unmutilated target—a tin can set on a post—like an enemy. It brought an indrawn somberness to his long bony face, not quite hardened to the lines of manhood. His eyes were gray as smoke, now faintly squinting under their heavy dark brows. Above a high forehead his shock of black hair was roached like a mule's mane. His chin was stubborn and with his full lower lip conspired to lend a hungry brooding to his expression even in repose.

Point your gun like a finger, Jesse had always said. *Aim by feel but give yourself that second. You ain't J. E. B. Stuart; just see you get there with the mostest.*

The gun, blurring up and coming level, sent whipcrack echoes across the silent yard, and the can leaped up and bounded away into the empty breaking corral; and sighting between the poles Calem sent it another twenty feet. His third shot dropped the can, dented and twisted, into a bed of trampled mud. He lowered the gun and licked his lip and blinked against the stench of powdersmoke; he grinned again.

The rattle of the wagon coming up by the pasture gate froze Calem then, and he tore his shirt open and rammed the gun inside. Not

2

looking around, he set off toward the tack barn with his hands in his pockets, a casual whistle on his lips. But his belly was turning hot and cold; they couldn't have failed to hear those three shots. He had learned to speak softly and mind his talk or else he would have sworn. It was hardly past noon, and most Saturdays they would lay over in town till nearly nightfall.

Ducking into the barn and its shadows, Calem pulled out the gun and jammed it into an open barrel of grain. As he stepped outside, the spring wagon was swinging past, and his father gave him a hard sideglance, his iron-colored eyes stabbing him. His gut tightening more, Calem walked slowly toward the house. His father reined up the team by the slanting lean-to near the kitchen door and climbed stiffly down. After assisting his wife to the ground, he turned wordlessly, ignoring her low anxious, 'Jared,' and came straight on toward his son.

Jared Gault was a tall and rawboned man, gaunt and dry and unbent, and his drab linsey shirt and homespun jeans hung on him like tattered cast-offs on a scarecrow. He was ungainly but not ludicrous; the hard strength of him thrust out at you from his deeply lined, deeply weathered face. He came to a stop and planted his run-down workboots a little apart, and Calem halted too.

Jared said briefly, 'Where is the gun, boy?'

3

'In the barn.'

Jared's big-knuckled hand made a motion, and Calem turned and tramped ahead of him. In the barn he dug deep in the feed barrel, feeling for the gun, and brought it out. Jared took it, handling it like something unclean, and laid it on a bench. He straightened.

'Where did you get it?'

'From Jesse before he lit out.'

Jared's breath whistled out gently. 'A good two years ago, then. And the shells?'

Calem's face was warm, and he lowered his eyes.

'Reckoned I'd missed a few time to time. My rifle gun shells would fit this one. Never heard a shot, though.'

'I—' Calem made a loose gesture. 'That place Jesse and I used to go back in the hills—uh—shot it off there some . . .'

'Bare your back.'

'Pa—'

'Bare your back, son.' Jared's eyes were strangely tired. Calem met his stare a long moment and, slowly turning, peeled off his shirt and planted his palms against the wall. A shame boiled in his belly. It had been four years since Pa had used the strap. He heard him cross the barn to some harness hanging on the wall, then a rattle of dry leather, and Jared came up behind him. He shut his eyes. The first blow drew a grunt from him, and then Calem clamped his teeth and braced out nine

4

more strokes without a wince, counting them by old habit and letting his breath sigh out on the last one. After he had shrugged carefully into his shirt and buttoned it, his father picked up the gun and said curtly, 'Come along,' and wheeled outside. Halting, he pulled back his arm and threw the gun. It made a bright arc in the sun and struck the sod in the horse pasture and bounced twice.

'Let it rust there ... Why, Calem?' There was a first break in Gault's voice, and slowly he shook his head from side to side. 'Can you tell me why?'

'No, Pa.'

'It's a possibility,' Jared said gently, 'that I told you too long ago for it to take good. A handgun ain't like a rifle, which can be took up for the use of killing your game or your varmints. Worse coming to worse, you can defend yourself with a rifle. But a man packs a sidearm is one priming for trouble when there is no goddam need.' It was his strongest oath, yet infrequently used, and his face was ruddy with anger. 'I rode with Quantrill and with George Todd and "Bloody Bill" Anderson. And with Cole Younger and Frank James and his slimy little brother "Dingus". Him you heard called Jesse, and giving your brother that name was never my notion. I knew 'em all. They used to string Navy Colts from their belts like beads. I saw—' Jared broke off, his breathing ragged, and Calem watched him

5

open-mouthed. 'I never told you none of that, and don't mean to. All you got to mind is that I joined up a green kid and it took me a while to learn the difference between a soldier and a wild-eyed killer. I quit the band after Jeff Davis outlawed Quantrill in '63, and spent ever since burying it to my own mind. I told Jesse some of it, but I reckon not enough to make the difference.'

'You pushed him!' Calem let it out in hot protest, saying the words at last.

'What was that?' Jared took a step and balled his son's shirtfront in a fist, shaking him savagely. 'By God, that's your mother talking! Don't you ever—'

He broke off and said, 'Ahhh,' with a soft and bitter note, pushing Calem away. 'Let it take, boy. A licking never broke the sap from Jesse, and I don't expect it will from you. Too much of me in you both. But you ain't like your brother; you got a mind and you got ears. Use 'em, and mind what I said. Let it take, Calem.'

He wheeled and strode toward the house, and Calem trudged slowly after him. He knew his father was a hard man, not a brutal one; the harsh and the gentle warred in him and the mixture was confusing. *Quantrill.* Did that explain things? Calem understood Jared enough to have doubted him only once: no man could halter-break a colt with a gentler hand, yet he had dealt only a harsh and unforgiving one to his older son. Martha

6

Gault, understanding her husband still better, had shared that doubt, and her forgiveness of him after the explosive final quarrel that drove Jesse away for good had come hard.

Still, Jesse's wildness had been brash and unrepentant; there was always some girl, but that was the least of it. He'd had a talent for slithering out of that sort of trouble; it was his wounding of a drunken and belligerent cowhand in a saloon brawl that had broken his father's patience.

They hadn't seen him since, and range gossip carried only vague rumors, but they knew he was hanging with a wild bunch over by Pima Flats, not far east. Only last week one of the bunch had been hanged as a proven rustler.

Jared Gault only clamped his jaw against such talk, having forbidden Jesse's name to be mentioned under his roof.

Calem's mother was waiting in the doorway. She was a large woman on the stout side with gray hair bunned tightly on her head. Over the years some of her husband's iron had rubbed into her square, stern face. The gentleness was in her eyes, her quiet voice.

'Come in, Calem, and take off your shirt.'

Jared, hoisting a sack of flour out of the wagon bed, said with a frown, 'First he'll help me tote this stuff in the lean-to.'

Her mouth tightened. 'No, Mr. Gault. No.'

Their life together was a good one, with all

differences met by a measured compromise, and Jared, in whipping his son, had had his way. Now it was Martha Gault's turn. Jared shrugged a wry concession, heaved the sack to his shoulder and tramped into the lean-to.

Calem sat at the table, his arms tightly folded, while Martha bathed his back with hot water which brought every welt alive till she applied the cool relief of a salve. Jared came in, took off his black slouch hat and hung it up. 'There was no need to shame him so.' Martha was calmly reproachful, walking to the doorway to throw out the basin water. 'He's a man now, Mr. Gault.'

Jared said irritably, 'Then let him act the man,' and sat down, leaning an elbow on the table and rubbing a hand over his face. 'Damn it all, Martha.'

'You push too hard, Mr. Gault,' she said and compressed her lips.

They ate the dinner of beef and biscuits and wilted greens in silence. Afterward Jared took out his stubby, blackened pipe and struck a match. 'You find time away from your various interests to do the chores I told you?' Calem muttered yes. Jared frowned into his pipebowl, coaxing it alight. 'That's something. I do appreciate your industry, boy.' He got the pipe going and drowned the match in his coffee dregs. 'Cut the marketing short today so we could get to that fencing.'

Martha clattered some soiled dishes into the

washpan. 'Blue Horse Spring?' A worried note crept into her voice. 'I thought you weren't decided.'

'I've put it off long enough.' Jared rose and walked to the door and took down his hat. 'If there's to be trouble, might as well have it done with.'

Without a word she went to the east wall and lifted his rifle from its pegs. 'No, Martha.' Jared cleared his throat gently. 'That there's looking for it. We will wait till the fence is up and see.' He clamped his hat on decisively and walked out.

Calem gulped his coffee, wiped his mouth, and stood. His mother held out the rifle. 'Take it, Calem.' He hesitated, and she said, 'Take it along. He takes a spell building a head of steam. It's gone off now.'

He took the rifle, opened the breech and checked the load, and looked at her. 'Take care, Calem,' she said softly, and he sensed the depth of her worry.

She had reason for it. There were few fences in Coyotero Basin; good watering places were far between, and by tacit agreement the basin ranchers left them open so that no man's cattle would be slacked. Blue Horse Spring lay on the line between the hardscrabble Gault outfit and Major Jeffrey Dembrow's big, sprawling Skull to the north. There had never been trouble over watering rights there because Skull's northwest range was hard by the only abundant water in the basin, Ten Mile Tanks below Mesa Amarillo. But after a band of Coyotero Apaches, reservation breakaways, had made camp near the mesa a month ago, Major Dembrow had been pushing his far-drifting stock south toward safer range and water, including Blue Horse Spring. His thirsty cattle had trampled the spring that supported the meager Gault herd to a muddy mire.

Jared Gault had not pleaded but had made his case clear to the Major. Jeffrey Dembrow, an oldtime cavalryman, had a ramrod will to match his small, hard body. His reply of 'We'll see,' had held a spare indifference, and his real answer had been to throw more cows into the Blue Horse area. That was when Jared Gault, a man with iron of its own sort tempered by a hatred of violence, had toyed with the notion of fencing off the spring. Now his decision was solid, making an acid test of how far the Major would go.

Calem said, 'Don't worry, Ma,' trying to lard it with conviction, and went outside on the lope. He jumped into the bed of the wagon as his father drove it across the yard. Stacked by the barn was a pile of fresh-cut cedar posts that had been intended for pasture fencing. Jared halted the team and stepped down, only then noting the rifle. He scowled but said nothing. They loaded the posts. Jared fetched two rolls of new wire from the barn, while

Calem toted out the shovels, wire stretchers and pliers, two hammers and a keg of staples. He sat the seat with the rifle on his knees and Jared grimly hoorawed the team into motion.

Calem breathed deeply of the hot afternoon, trying to ease the knot of trouble in him. A hawk spiraled against the glittering sky; wind flattened the brown grass of the rolling flats in undulant waves, and to the north rose the red hulk of Mesa Amarillo and, beyond, the serrated dark tracery of mountains. That far range was as virgin and untamed to his mind as when his grandfather, Ephraim Gault, had tramped and trapped it with 'Old Bill' Williams, Tom Fitzpatrick, Bridger and old Glass and the young Kit Carson. And he remembered the long winter evenings by a roaring fire in the Missouri farmhouse, he and Jesse hugging their knees, wide-eyed while the old mountain man told of the Shining Mountains of his youth, the big beaver kills and piles of glistening 'plew,' the red-eyed rendezvous and ring-tailed eye-gouging *hivernants*. At which their mother shortly dispatched the boys to bed, but Jesse and Calem would lie awake for hours, whispering, dreaming out loud.

The wild flavor of it stayed with Calem, and it must have taken to a degree with Jared too, for he'd pulled his stakes, westering shortly after Gramps died. But Jared was a plodding sort of man, stolid and close-mouthed of his

11

desires, the impractical dreamer offset by the family provider. If there was a bloodstrain of wildness in the Gaults, it had cropped out strongly in Jesse, while in Calem it was a qualified rebellion against not his father's settled ways but his rutted notions. A keen but untutored mind not yet come to terms with itself might find a restless outlet in gun practice, but it was also a thinking mind aware of duty; his father and mother, no longer young, needed his strong back—and more.

Calem started, wrenched from his reverie, as Jared spoke suddenly: 'Don't think too hard of me, son. Maybe I took the wrong tack with Jesse, though I'll larrup you if you tell your ma I said so. Jess—' he paused, picking his words with difficulty—'he always had to act black when you said white. Harder you tugged, the more he shied. I was hellfire on loose women, so he took all he could find. Called a pistol the devil's own tool, so he took to one like a duck takes to water.' His jaw ridged hard against its black stubble. 'Had to be a way of handling Jess, but I never found it.'

Jared was silent for a time, then: 'I know you been wanting to cut the traces. Got an idea why you ain't too, and want to say I am obliged. Ain't forgot how a colt's vinegar boils sometime.' He cleared his throat and closed his mouth, and Calem respected his embarrassment. Today had seen breaks in Jared's gruff and indrawn reserve, and these

12

words had cost him an effort.

Shortly the wagon left the flats for humpy grass knolls. Jared negotiated the jolting wagon expertly, braking down a long flank into the muddy vale where Blue Horse Spring lay. It was a natural saucer about a hundred feet in diameter. The water, once clear and pure, was brown and roiled and stood in glassy pools in the trampled hoofpocks around the edge. A number of cattle stood about muzzling the dirty water, and these moved off sluggishly at their approach. Some yards back the caked mud had baked to a laved whiteness seamed with a network of cracks. Here Jared halted, got down and tramped through the loose mud to the spring. He stared at it a bitter moment; his orders were brief and harsh, and they went to work.

They dug and sweated for two hours under the broiling sun, and Calem decided that spading postholes through slushy mud and the solid hardpan beneath was as mean a chore as he'd known. They had thirty feet of cedar posts anchored when, pausing for a breather, he saw the lone rider watching from a hillcrest. He said, 'Pa,' and Jared growled without looking up, 'I see him.' The rider soon cantered off the hill and was gone.

Calem was watchful after that, and he said nothing when two more horsemen skylined into view and came straight on toward the spring. Jared rammed his shovel into the

13

ground and sleeved his forehead on his grimy shirtarm, waiting. The two men came around the spring, skirting the mud, and halted. Ed Grymes, the Skull foreman, said meagerly, 'Boots Hostettor was riding line and seen you. Good thing for you, Gault.'

The weathertracks deepened around Jared's eyes. 'How you figure?'

'Save you plenty more work. Them posts is coming down.'

Calem edged backward toward the wagon, and Jared said mildly, 'No, none of that. Hold still, Calem.'

Grymes' stare passed from Calem to the rifle on the wagon seat, and he gave a bleak nod. 'Smart. No call for it.'

He was a massive barrel of a man with a moon face whose bland dullness was relieved by a full black cavalry mustache. His reputation for toughness was less a bone-deep quality of his than part of the front that went with overseeing the affairs of a big outfit, and his loyalty to Skull was deep and doglike and unswerving.

Ames Dembrow said impatiently, 'Let's get to it, Ed.' He was Major Dembrow's only son, a wire-tempered man in his mid-twenties, slim as a whip. His mouth was hard in the way of a cruel-bitted horse's, but he was a wan mirror of his father. He wore *taja* leggings, a fancy charro jacket, and a black Spanish hat with a band of silver conches, which also decorated

14

his fine black saddle.

Grymes rumbled, 'No call to crowd it yet,' as he swung heavily to the ground, his bleached eyes watchful on Jared. 'Gault, we'll give you a hand.'

Jared planted his feet apart, and his big fists knotted against his thighs; his answer came low and flat. 'No. Them posts stay up. I had enough.'

Grymes cuffed his hat back with a swipe of his fist, scowling at the line of posts. 'Sorry about this. Thought the Major'd made it plain enough. Ten Mile Springs is too close to them Coyoteroes. After they move on—'

'Them Coyoteroes ain't touched the basin cattle,' Jared broke in heatedly. 'They ain't wartrailing; they want to be left alone, live their own way. That goes for me. But how long you think my cows can live on this slop? Blue Horse can't water half your herd too.' He pointed a long arm. 'I'll leave it open there. With the spring fenced you can water your stock a small bunch at a time. After they're in shape to move, you can drive 'em on. There's other places on Skull.'

Ames Dembrow said softly, 'Told you, Ed. This brush-hopper's got to be showed.' He reined abruptly sideways, lifting his coiled rope off his pommel; he shook out a loop and dabbed it over a post and heeled off to take up the slack.

As quickly, Jared took six long steps, butting

Grymes aside with the heel of his palm; he reached Dembrow and caught his belt and yanked sideways, dumping him to the ground. Almost in the same motion he wheeled away and slogged to the post, jerking slack into the taut noose to lift it off.

Ames Dembrow, sprawled on his side in the muck, raised his head. His hat had fallen off and his long blond hair hung over his mud-smeared cheek. His eyes blazed with bad temper, and seeing the gun come up in his fist, Calem stood rooted and dumb. Grymes spun toward Ames now, yelling, 'No!'

The gunroar cut his words in half.

Jared Gault, coming about on his heel then, took the shot full in the chest, and the impact arched him backward. Falling, his body had a boneless looseness even before it struck the mud.

Calem stood in a shocked detachment, watching Ames Dembrow crawl to his knees. 'Now,' Ames said in a hot and shaking voice, 'we're tearing down those posts.'

CHAPTER TWO

Calem tramped out of the Coyotero County courthouse like a sleepwalking man, his mind closed to the bustle of Saturday traffic. He halted, blinking at the harsh midday sunlight, and his mother's hand tightened on his arm; she murmured, 'Calem.'

He said, 'All right,' and assisted her to the high seat of their wagon. People were straggling from the courthouse in loose groups, talking as they headed for saloons and stores. The tie rails were lined with rigs and single horses, and like others on a long market-and-court day, the Gaults' team had been unhitched and tied to the tailgate so that the horses could feed on straw in the wagon bed.

Calem walked to the tailgate to untie the team, and now a burst of laughter pulled his glance to the courthouse entrance. Ames Dembrow had stepped out, passing talk with some friends. He paused on the steps, hipcocked and wearing his dark suit with a slim grace, and took out a cigar. Briefly, as he bit off the end of the cigar, his light restless eyes locked Calem's. The arrogant humor in his handsome face hardened into open mockery as he spat out the cigartip.

Ames' young wife lagged behind him, a bored indifference in her face, and he glanced at her with a sharp word. She moved dutifully forward, taking his arm, and Ames deliberately lighted his cigar and chuckled at something a friend had said. *We're Dembrows*, his whole manner said with a hard conviction, *and we are not required to give a damn*. The party moved on down the sidewalk, talking and laughing.

17

Ed Grymes came out now, edging along ponderously, almost furtively, behind a wedge of other people. Martha Gault said calmly, 'Mr. Grymes.' Her tone was even, almost underpitched, yet it cut through a hubbub of talk. People hauled up, looking on curiously.

Grymes said unsteadily, 'Miz Gault—'

'Why did you lie, Mr. Grymes?'

'No, ma'am'—he was already shaking his head—'no, ma'am,' and came off the steps with his head hunched, walking swiftly to his tied horse. Swinging up, he roweled the animal away with a furious haste. The undercurrent of talk resumed as the onlookers broke up, and Calem hitched the team.

He had swung to the seat to take up the reins when Major Dembrow and his nephew Cody came out of the courthouse, apparently the last to leave. Cody had started to say something, but the Major cut him off with a lifted hand and came over to the wagon, doffing his hat.

Jeffrey Dembrow was not a big man, and his head was outsize for his body, which was blocky and compact, but his square face was stamped with the habit of command. His full face was strongly handsome, while a Roman senator might have envied his profile; his crisp plume of white hair was peaked at the temples with small devil's horns that seemed to bristle with his moods. It made a solid contrast to his black brows, arched above a single eye of flinty

18

gray; the other being covered by a black eyepatch. That eye, with a trick way of seeming to look beyond whatever it fixed, gave him a distance and austerity heightened by the black broadcloth he usually wore, but lessened by a sensitive, mobile mouth that betrayed a driving impatience coldly restrained.

'Ma'am,' he said quietly, 'I deeply regret the ordeal this matter has caused you—and even the necessity for it. I would like you to know that.'

'It's heard.' Martha Gault kept her eyes directly on the team. 'Drive along, Calem.' It was an utter dismissal of Major Dembrow and whatever charitable suggestions he might offer. He stepped back with a stiff bow and turned away.

Calem set a brisk clip on the south road, heading home. A searching sideglance at his mother showed him a stern composure in her face, her hands folded on the lap of her black dress. Her forty-five years of living had never offered her an easy lot, and absorbing the fact of Jared's death could only strengthen her care-tempered dignity. Calm and dry-eyed since the first shock had spent itself, she had gone through the motions of a service, a funeral, an inquest and now an open hearing as a matter of course. Because Calem knew that her callous if simple acceptance was anything but unfeeling, it awed him a little.

For him, unable till now to shake the

strange numb unreality of the shooting and all that followed, it was only beginning. He had a memory like a bad taste of how he had only stood, dumbly unmoving after Ames Dembrow rode away, until Ed Grymes had stirred him with a brusque order. Together they had lifted his father's body to the wagon and he had driven it home, feeling like an observer in a bad dream from which there was no pinching yourself awake. That tough and vital Jared, who should have been good for his own father's fourscore and five, was suddenly a broken and lifeless lump in the mud had made no sense at all. Maybe it was only a vacuum of personal helplessness, of apathy reinforced by taking for granted that justice would be done and all of it was out of his hands.

Today the court hearing had shown otherwise, and now like a forming crack in the dike of bewildered disbelief, anger was trickling through, black and bitter and scouring. Ames Dembrow had good reason for his bland cocksureness, and knowing only this, Calem let the mounting fury have its free, unreasoning way with his thoughts.

The five miles rolled behind them without talk until they turned through the pasture gate below the house. Martha shaded her eyes, peering toward the porch. 'Seems we've company. Reckon a neighbor come to pay his respects.'

Calem muttered, 'Took him long enough,'

and then hauled up the team abruptly, his heart lifting to his throat. The man sitting in deep shadow on the porch had stood, and now with a slack negligence he stepped off the porch. Calem said softly, 'Ma,' and heard the sharp catch in her breath.

Letting out a whoop, he rein-whipped the team into a run. 'Calem,' she protested, 'don't drive so—oh, Jess. Jesse! . . .'

An hour later, sitting at slack after-dinner ease and picking his teeth, Jesse Gault was saying, 'That's about it, Ma. I cut the dust out of Pima Flats without delay soon as I got the news about Pa from this drifting man. Sorry to miss the funeral.'

Martha's eyes glowed with a softness that Calem hadn't seen in a long time. 'It's all right. You're home, Jesse.'

Jesse selected a nut from a table-centered bowl and cracked it between the heels of his palms. 'Sure, Ma.' He punched Calem lightly on the arm, chewing and grinning. 'Boy, you sure enough grown a damn foot.' The old deviltry filled his dark eyes, and except for a veneer of cool assurance he hadn't changed by a jot. His long saturnine face beneath his roached black hair was smooth and unlined. A faint white scar showed in the deeply weathered skin of his forehead, and his left ear was thickened by scar tissue. Otherwise he was the old Jesse, slim and hard, with a lazy grace about him, and Calem felt a surge of warm

21

feeling. Jesse was back and now, somehow, things had to be all right.

'So you testified at a hearing today?' Jesse tilted back his head, tossing the nutmeat into his mouth. 'How she go, boy?'

Calem's warm moment went cold, and his voice thickened with resurging wrath as he talked. 'He said Pa grabbed his rifle after knocking Ames off his horse. Like Ames had no choice, and that's how it goes in the record.'

'I can't believe it,' Martha said quietly. 'Ed Grymes helped Calem bring Jared home. He told me himself how it had happened, and it wasn't easy for him.'

'Look, Ma, Ed is Skull ranch. So is Ames, and the Major's whelp into the bargain. Hell, it's sewed up.' Jesse tilted back his chair, grinning with a hard wisdom. 'The word of the Skull foreman against a two-bit cattleman's grieving son? Take it to trial and any good shyster will have tall medicine out of making Cal all unwrought by Pa's death. Grymes is not a bad sort for all he's stupid as an ox, but he's Skull and that comes first.'

Martha said heatedly, 'Don't talk like that. There has to be a way, Jesse.'

'Look, Ma.' Jesse cracked another nut, scowling. 'You don't live in the world the preacher tells about at Sunday meeting, the one you want to believe in. You're in the real one where right and wrong don't mean worth a damn.' A faint jeer touched his lips. 'You want

22

to find out what you don't have the belly for, you people, take it all the way to trial and watch a man guilty as hell walk free.' He popped the nutmeat into his mouth. 'That's if you could get it to trial.'

'No,' Martha said softly, stubbornly. 'That's your world, I know, but it's not mine. I can't accept that Jared's killer will go unpunished. There has to be a way.'

'A way,' Calem echoed bitterly. 'There's one way for sure, and it's past time someone said it.'

He saw the small shock in her eyes, and then Jesse said swiftly, 'He don't mean it, Ma,' as he stabbed a hard finger against Calem's arm. 'You listen, boy. Go after that Dembrow now or ever and you'll kick up a wildcat that'll tear you apart.'

'I can take him,' Calem said hotly. 'I can handle a gun with you, Jess! You ain't seen me!'

'I don't want to,' Jesse said coldly. 'That's my style, maybe, but not yours. If something happens to you, what'll happen to Ma? You think on that!'

'All right, it's your style! You take him—you hadn't no plans on staying around anyway, Jess, that ain't your style either. So you take him and drift!'

Jesse stood swiftly and stalked to the window, staring out. His voice came tight and hard. 'All right, I'll say it. I didn't want to, for

23

Ma's sake, but I will. My old man's dead, and you know how much that meant to me? It meant I could come home and see my mother.' He leaned his hands on the window frame, breathing heavily. 'I took his switch lickings and his hard talk for rough on twenty years, and if there was a kindly word in any of it, I don't recall it. I don't hate him no more, fact I don't feel a damn thing. Happen otherwise, I might not sit about on my hands, but that's how it is.' He dropped his arms and turned, shaking his head. 'I didn't want to say that, Ma.'

'Neither of you could help the way you was,' Martha said tiredly. 'Born or made, Jess, there's nothing a body can forgive in that. I'm as glad, if it'll stop more killing. I'd as lief leave Jared's killer to God, come to that. You, Calem, you listen to your brother.'

'What about our water rights?' Calem demanded. 'Skull will hold Blue Horse now, and where'll we water?'

Jesse said acidly, 'You reckon bracing Dembrow will help that?'

Calem ducked his head stubbornly, biting his lip. Jesse moved back to his chair, lifted a foot to it and leaned his elbow on his knee, gently shaking his finger. 'You hear me now, and hear good. You and Ma sell the place for what you can get and head back to Missouri. We got family there, and they'll help you get a fresh start.' His voice hardened distinctly. 'But

24

get shed of your damfool notion or I'll trim it out of you.'

'I'd like to be back with my own,' Martha said wistfully. 'Coming to New Mexico was Jared's want. But he put so many years, so much work into this place, and I feel—'

'Look at the facts,' Jesse said impatiently. 'If you hang on here, the Dembrows will crowd you out. Even with good water, Cal couldn't work the outfit alone.'

'No. But you, Jesse?'

He gave a wry shrug. 'You know me, Ma. I gather no moss.'

'I know.' Martha Gault sighed. 'Well, Bart Renshaw—he owns the place next ours on the south—wanted to buy us out a while back. Maybe . . .'

She talked on, the words washing distantly over Calem's head. Again he saw Jared lifeless in the mud, and he saw Ames Dembrow's light mocking eyes. He squeezed his fists beneath the table till they were bloodless. *I won't let it go by, Pa. By God, I won't.*

Jesse smoked three cigarettes through, listening and interjecting occasionally; then he swung to his feet. 'Come on, kid. I ain't seen the place in two years; how about a last look around?'

Calem shook his head tightly.

'Well, I got a few memories laying around, not all bad ones. Reckon I'll take a ride.' He picked up his hat, and then catching his mother's sharp eye, chuckled. 'Don't fret, Ma. My foot ain't that itchy. I can stay around anyway till you and Cal pull out.'

He left the house, and shortly Calem heard him ride away. He pushed back his chair then and stood, as Martha said gently, 'Son, don't brood on it now. You do think a sight about things, and given time you'll think deeper. No matter how bad it seems now, that will pass and you'll see your life ahead of you and know Jess was right.'

'Sure, Ma. It's all right.' He scrubbed a vague palm over his jaw. 'Better change my clothes and get to fixing that pasture fence.'

He went through the parlor to his room and changed from his stiff cheap suit into jeans and shirt. Then he dug a worn gunbelt and holster and a small handful of hoarded cartridges out of hiding. He stuffed them in his shirt and left the house, whistling. Reaching the horse pasture he ducked through the fence and sauntered along inside it, now and then leaning his weight to a post as if testing it. Presently he spotted the old gun in the grass where Jared had thrown it, brightly blued in the sunlight except for the flecks of dew rust. Putting his back to the house he bent in one swift casual motion and scooped up the gun, ramming it in his belt. Straightening then, careful not to look toward the house where his mother might be watching, he passed an idle glance over the south end of the pasture which was cut off from the house by the tack barn. The big lineback buckskin Jared had always used for a saddle mount was grazing there.

Calem continued along the fence, not hurrying, till he was past the corner of the barn. He ducked in through the rear door and took Jared's rig and rope from the saddle pole, sweating in his haste. Five minutes later the buckskin was ready, fretting at the bit as Calem led him toward the south gate. Once more he was in full view of the house, and as he opened the gate, heard the sharp lift of his mother's voice: 'Calem—Calem!'

He didn't look back. Vaulting to the saddle, he heeled the buckskin into a stretching run on the town road.

CHAPTER THREE

Cody Dembrow stepped from the China Cafe and halted on the sidewalk to light his cheap cigar; he stepped to the edge of the walk and teetered there on the high heels of his run-down cowman's boots, thumbs tucked in his vest pockets. Cody was a big man of twenty-seven, his chest and shoulders heavy with a quilting of muscle that strained the seams of his old suitcoat. His face was broad and ruddy, crowned by a stiff cap of close-cropped blond hair. It was a pleasant face, though bland

27

almost to indifference, finding a kind of negative redemption in his deep-lidded eyes which lent an expression both sly and sleepy.

He half-turned, hearing the door of the cafe open behind him. Jeffrey Dembrow stepped out with his daughter-in-law, his arm bent with a stately courtesy where her hand rested. 'I'll bring the buggy from the livery barn, my dear,' the Major was saying. A burst of laughter rolled out behind him; the Major's snowy brows drew together in a frown as he glanced through the half-frosted front window at the counter inside, where his son was joking and roughnecking with some town friends. Then he gave Cody a curt nod. 'Ready to leave, or would you prefer to drink the Silver Belle dry with Ames?'

'I'll go home with you, sir.'

'Stay with Trenna, please, and I'll bring the buggy here from the livery barn, and your horse as well.'

Cody watched his uncle quarter across the street at an angry walk. Ordinarily Cody would be assigned a chore like mount-fetching, but at the moment deeply offended by the apple of his eye, the Major had no wish to wait in earshot of Ames' raucous exuberance. Full of high spirits after the inquest, Ames had not shared their table in the cafe; he had joined his friends with loud and occasionally foul talk.

Cody gave Trenna an appraising glance; her face gave no hint of her feelings. Ames' wife,

28

like any of his string of thoroughbred horses, was a sleek fine animal, tall and full-bodied in a blue serge habit that set off her skydeep eyes. A matching hat jauntily topped her pale hair; her slim heartshaped face was serene except for the shadow of discontent marring its full mouth.

Cody hadn't stirred, and now Trenna stepped to his side and took his arm; her look was chiding. 'Not noted for gallantry, are you, my friend?'

Cody smiled faintly. 'Is that what you want?'

Her hand tightened on his arm. 'You know better,' she murmured. 'No, I'd settle for some simple attention. It's the first time in two months I've been in town. I wouldn't be now if it weren't court day for the Dembrows and we-all had to put in an appearance to publicly demonstrate our solidarity behind Ames' and Grymes' lying testimony.'

'Now,' Cody said dryly, 'don't tell me that Ames told you he and Grymes were lying.'

She gave a short, deprecating laugh. 'Ames tells me nothing. You saw that Gault boy testify. Didn't it occur to you he was telling the simple truth about what happened at Blue Horse?'

'I couldn't say.'

'You mean you won't. You never commit yourself till you see your way, do you, Cody?'

'No.'

She laughed quietly. 'I watched young

Gault's face when Ames and Grymes gave testimony; that boy is wound up like a watchspring, and some of it broke through then. Ames, after all, is perfectly capable of killing a man in cold blood—or hot. Oh yes, they were lying.'

That could be, Cody thought almost indifferently; Ed Grymes was enough scared of Ames to cover for him. 'Do you care?'

'No more than you.' Her blue stare behind a wisp of veil held a disturbing intensity, and he had a vivid memory of the first time he had seen her, a percentage queen in a trail town where he and Ames had been on a cattle-buying trip. Ames had brought her back to Skull as his bride. Her poise, diction and aristocratic beauty let Cody concede her a good background, but she had obviously taken a long slip. Still, a beautiful and cultured woman who could fit the role demanded by Major Dembrow of his son's wife was rare, and Ames, whose tastes ran to high-class bordellos, would not be inclined to look far. Trenna satisfied the Major's standards outwardly, and he'd never questioned the rest.

Still holding his eyes, she said softly, 'He'll be in town all day. We can have the whole afternoon—the usual place.'

Cody hesitated; the challenge of her vivid allure was strong, warring with his innate caution. She was a bored and restless woman, and he understood her resentment. Ames kept her virtually locked away, as he would any prized possession. She could have anything she wanted, but a dozen expensive ball gowns that she could wear no place meant nothing. From the first Cody had recognized her as his own kind, and living under the same roof had made an attraction inevitable. But their secret meetings were few and far between, confined by Cody's careful nature. The honor of his household was a thing the Major took for granted, as he took his own honor; it was a vague conviction of Ames' suspicions that underscored Cody's growing unease about the clandestine affair. And he shook his head.

She whispered, 'Coward,' but they fell silent as Ames came out of the cafe. He halted behind them, and Cody felt the back of his neck prickle under Ames' stare. Ames said nothing, and the three of them watched the currents of life along the street while silence stretched thin between them.

Cody felt a swift relief as the buggy rattled upstreet from the livery barn. The Major halted the matched bays; Cody assisted Trenna to the high seat by the Major, then stepped behind the vehicle where his saddled horse was tied. The Major shot an impatient glance at his son. 'You can fetch your own horse.'

'Not just yet,' Ames murmured. He stood hipshot, working a toothpick in the corner of his mouth. 'You take Trenna home, Pa. I want to make big medicine with Cody over to the

Silver Belle.'

'As you wish.' The Major clucked the team into motion, and Cody felt a shadowy anxiety in Trenna's swift glance at him before the wagon rolled on. Without another word Ames started across the street; Cody followed, a deep worry thickening his throat now. He left his sorrel at the Silver Belle tierail where one other mount bearing the Skull brand stood. As they went through the batwing doors, Ames said curtly, 'Get a bottle and join me,' and headed for a far corner table.

A cool gloom and a stale memory of whiskey and stratified smoke clung to the long high room, deserted except for the bartender and Frenchy Duval, who broke off their idle talk as Cody moved to the bar. The Silver Belle was a cowman's watering place, unfrequented by the Saturday town crowd of family men. It would come to life tonight when the cattle crews hit town to tie knots in the wildcat's tail.

Frenchy Duval gave a polite nod. 'You will have the drink on me, my friend, eh?' Duval was gaunt as a wolf, with a pinched face and slitted saffron eyes. His black hair was done in a thin queue down the side of his head, and he contrived to wear his shabby range clothes with a trace of Gallic elegance.

Cody shook his head. 'Maybe later. A bottle, Len. Skull credit.'

Duval briefly turned his yellow stare on

Ames and nodded his understanding. *He sees a sight more than he lets on*, Cody thought, remembering all he knew of Duval. He was a Cajun who had punched cows on the Louisiana side of the Sabine; later he had run with a gang of border rustlers down near Brownsville, Texas, where he had three known killings to his credit. Here in Coyotero Basin he had handled more than one minor range dispute for Major Dembrow that never reached court. His air of wolfish danger was enough to quell a dispute, and today an uncertainty of public sympathy in the Gault killing had prompted the Major to bring Duval along to town.

Cody carried the bottle and a pair of glasses to the rear table, toed out a chair and sat. 'Pour me a drink,' Ames told him stonily, and he poured it. Ames took his drink, then drew a long nine from his vest pocket and bit away the end and said, 'Give me a light.' Cody struck a match and held it. 'Now,' Ames exhaled deeply, 'I would admire to hear exactly what you're cooking up between you.'

'Trenna?' Cody said carefully. 'She wanted to talk was all. No harm in that.'

'I wonder,' Ames murmured, his eyes squinted against the smoke. 'I call it a pure caution, what-all the two of you find to talk about so frequent. Yes sir, now that could be a case.'

'Ames, there's nothing there—'

'Shut up.' Ames had closed his fist around the bottle, and the knuckles were white. 'You walk too goddamned soft for my taste, Cody, and you always have. I haven't forgot what a sly bastard you was when we were kids, only you've got so sly you don't show it. Sly enough so I judge you'll keep your place, and what I seen was Trenna's notion. But a likely word to the sly—you're on sufferance at Skull, always. Being kin gives you a few privileges, but one word from me'll break you to thirty-and-found, and don't you by God forget it.'

Cody dropped his gaze to the glass he was turning between his fingers. The brassy taste of hatred was so strong in his mouth it almost sickened him, festering because he could never betray it by word or expression. It wasn't only that he, the illegitimate son of Major Jeffrey Dembrow's dead sister and an unknown father, had grown up a charity ward to his uncle's sense of brusque duty. The countless arrogant, bullying slights by his cousin Ames made a bitter etching in his memory. It had been that way since they were boys, when Ames had found that Cody, aware of his tenuous position, could be baited with small torments in the way a boy could bait a docile and uncomplaining dog. Ames was the origin of his hate, but it extended almost as strongly to the Major. For years he had worked furiously for a gesture of affection or approval, only to meet his austere uncle's total, absent indifference.

Cody was never quite sure why he stayed on, doggedly accepting a daily ration of slights and flaunted contempt. Part of it was the rut of simple habit, and he supposed that a man's knowledge of his bastardy could foster an obsession for real roots. Skull was the only home he knew, and perversely enough, that he wore the hated Dembrow name lent him a proprietary feeling toward the place. A feeling marred by the brooding fact that as things were, he belonged to it and not the other way around . . .

He lifted his eyes, meeting the goading mockery in Ames'; he thought, *There's more than one bastard at this table, but I'm the patient one. And one day I'll take you by the short hairs, cousin.*

Behind him the batwing doors rattled on their rockers as someone came in. Cody saw a visible start in Ames' eyes, and they narrowed slowly. Cody glanced backward over his shoulder as Frenchy Duval murmured, 'Well, well.'

It was the Gault kid, standing big and lean with his feet apart, and there was a wild and wicked light in his eyes. He wore a long-barreled conversion Walker in a tied-down holster, and there was a tension in his long arms. *He means business*, Cody thought narrowly, and when the kid put his stare on him and said flatly, 'You. Get off away from him,' Cody obeyed. He stood, carefully pulling back the skirt of his coat to show he was unarmed, and stepped aside.

Gault moved deeper into the room along the bar, keeping his eyes on the whole room, and stopped half-facing the bartender and Duval, who slid his wise glance from the gun Gault wore to the pure mulishness in his young face, and said softly again, 'Well, well.'

'What do you want here, kid?' the bartender asked mildly, dipping his big freckled hand casually below the bar. Cody remembered the bungstarter he kept there. But the kid stepped a wary sidepace from the bar, keeping his direct glance on Ames. Looking at Ames, seeing his mouth slightly open and his palms flat on the table, Cody thought, *He never expected this from a ragheel ranch kid.*

Frenchy Duval, his gaunt length slack against the bar, folded his arms with a quiet chuckle. 'Why don' you ask him what he wants, Ames, eh?'

'Sure,' Ames said softly. 'Sure.' Cody watched his cousin's hesitation fade to wary calculation, and then to grinning mockery as Ames said: 'How about it, Frenchy?'

The Cajun put all his expression into a minute shrug. 'Don' ask Frenchy; ask the boy.' At Ames' swift glance, he lifted the corners of his mouth. 'What you want of me, eh?'

'Not a damned thing. Sit tight.'

'Ah no—' Duval leisurely turned, his arms

36

still folded, and sauntered to the far end of the bar. 'A bullet don' go always where she should. I will stand here, I think.'

'You better,' Gault told him.

Duval's voice shook with laughter. 'Very quietly, my young rooster, but your neck will get wrung all the same—'

From the tail of his eye, Cody saw Ames' hands tense on the table. The kid's glance whipped back as Ames boiled out of his chair, heaving over the table; his fancy gun blurred out and up. Cody saw young Gault's hand slap his gunbutt, cock and bring up the heavy weapon in clean, easy reflex, taking a fleeting instant for aim as Ames sent off a wild bucking shot. Then Ames dived behind the upended table.

Cody knew then, with a peculiar and brittle clarity, how it would go, seeing the kid's wrist sinews tense for the solid jolt of squeezing off his shot, and seeing splinters fly from the table angled on its side by a broken leg. Cody saw Ames' face above it dark and contorted through a haze of powdersmoke. And Ames had not shot again. He was trying to get his feet under him, and now his hand stabbing out blindly struck the table and toppled it aside. Still on his knees, Ames hugged his hands to his chest and with a long, gurgling sigh, fell on his face.

It might have been five seconds before Gault, staring, remembered Duval. He

37

brought his gun jerkily to bear, but the Cajun was still slack-postured against the bar. Slowly Duval straightened, and walking to Ames, bent and turned him on his side. Afterward he looked at the ragged hole in the tabletop. He said softly, 'You are a great fool, my friend, but that was shooting.'

'Don't try anything,' Gault said in a high, strained voice.

'No, my young buck.' There was no laughter in Duval's face now. 'I have no fight with you. But soon Major Dembrow will give the order; there will be many men on the hunt. I have seen such things. Now you will run for a time, but we will meet again.'

Gault sidled to the door, shot a quick look over the batwings, and backed through them. Cody heard him cross the walk and scramble into his saddle, putting his horse in a dead run for the south end of town. A flurry of voices, lifted in curious excitement, was already gathering.

Stepping over to Ames, Cody saw that Gault's shot, fired through the table, had taken him in the center of the chest. He glanced at Duval, who shook his head and said, 'I would not have believe' this. Once I had the shooting game with Ames; he was good. Ver' good. Still he lost his head. The kid is a fool, but he was steady.'

Cody nodded, his eyes speculative. 'I'll handle things here. You ride after the Major and Mrs. Dembrow.'

Mention of Trenna made him realize that her problem was solved, or part of it was. He almost smiled then. Part of his too.

CHAPTER FOUR

Racing toward the town outskirts, Calem heard a shout and saw Bill Macavey, the town marshal, leaving his office at a waddling run. But Macavey's shout and his tub-bellied shape washed against Calem's senses in an empty blur, and then he passed the last building and lined onto the road, the thrumming of the buckskin's hoofs hammering in his temples like padded blows. For a straining mile he held the pace, fighting the thick burning in his guts. Finally, feeling it boil in his throat, he tight-reined the snorting lineback to a halt. He almost fell from the saddle, going on his hands and knees, and threw up. He thought, *Jess could have said how it would be*, and gulping, was sick again.

Shortly he took up the reins and shakingly mounted and rode on. He hadn't gone a half-mile when he made out a rider coming at a hard run across the flats, the tan dust roiling up in his wake. Calem halted again, and drew the Walker and laid it against his thigh, waiting. In a minute Jesse wheeled his slobbering black up beside him. 'What happened?'

When he had the story, Jesse said bitterly, 'All right, don't sit there. Follow me.'

Calem said sickly, 'Where?'

'Not home, they'll look there first. Our old place in the hills.'

Jesse led out as they left the road and angled southeast toward the dark timbered slopes that skirmished Coyotero Basin on the east. Calem watched the stiff angry set of his back for many minutes, and finally Jesse fell back beside him. 'How was it, kid?' A tight harshness strained the corners of his saturnine mouth. 'You like the taste of it?'

'Jess—'

'Shut up.' A gusty breath left Jesse, and he shook his head. 'You ain't cut from the same cloth as me, and you just had a taste of what that means. You think you know the rest too, but you don't. Kid, you don't know the half of it.'

He reined savagely out ahead once more, and they pushed into the deep hills. They forced their way through tangles of catclaw and manzanita that clung to the first rocky slopes, and then plunged into deep timber, putting their horses along a dim trail. Shortly they debouched onto an open clearing facing a granite cliff down which a mountain stream gushed in sheets of creamy spray and gathered in a deep pool before wending its way to the lowland.

Here they dismounted. Calem's legs felt rubbery, and he sat down abruptly on a rock and watched Jesse water the animals. He led them into a narrow well-grassed notch that thrust back deeply into the cliff, and returned presently carrying their saddlebags. Without a word he began to ascend the rock slide that fronted the lower cliff. Wearily, Calem got to his feet and followed him. The slide was steep-pitched, and rubble cascaded away beneath their boots. Halfway up, Jesse edged onto an abutting ledge which leaned above a vertical drop, and worked along it hugging the wall. After a few yards the ledge broadened and then sharply terminated, its rounded lip curving back into the cliff.

About four feet below the liprock was an opening less than a yard in diameter. They had discovered the cave years ago while hunting hereabouts, and it became a secret retreat where two boys could cache their small possessions or camp of a night. The entrance was invisible from the facing side of the cliff and from directly below. It penetrated at a side angle into the solid rock, and from below a body could see it only by hugging the cliff a good distance away and craning his neck. The one way of ingress was to let yourself bodily over the ledge while someone held your wrists, feel for the hole with your feet and worm yourself in. You reached up and supported

41

your partner as he precariously lowered himself by gripping the liprock.

They did the old maneuver easily, and then Calem struck a match. They negotiated a low narrow tunnel on their hands and knees, turned a sharp angle of it and came into an arching, sand-floored cavern. Jesse opened a saddlebag and took out a candle which he stuck upright in the sand. Calem lighted the wick as the match singed his fingers; he swore and dropped it.

'The old place,' Jesse murmured as the sallow light flickered over the rugged walls. 'How long, kid?'

'Six years. Never could get in here by my lonesome.'

Jesse grunted, digging his heel at something covered by dirt. He chuckled as he unearthed a corroded knifeblade. 'My old "Barlow", sure enough. Always wondered where I misput it.'

The bleak shape of the present faded momentarily in thoughts of a shared past, of long and carefree summer days playing and hunting, of swimming bare-butt in the icy pool, of the nights by a roaring fire down below cooking the grub they had packed or shot or snared, of the hours of talk in the dark cave snug and unworried in their blankets fancying all breeds of nocturnal menace and knowing they were high and safe from all.

Jesse sank with a grunt on his hunkers and settled his back to the wall. The bad light made a gaunt limning of his long face, as he sifted tobacco into a paper. 'Have yourself some rest, Deadeye. You're like to get precious little of that later on.'

Calem eased down beside him. 'Jess . . . what now?'

'We wait.' He jerked the drawstring of his Durham sack with his teeth, dropped it in his pocket, and rolled and sealed his smoke. 'Ma saddled up and caught up with me after you took out. Told her I'd bring you back tied to your saddle—alive, I hoped—else if it wasn't best we show up, to wait a day and come here. She knows the place.'

Calem gnawed his lip. 'Jess, you reckon she'll be all right?'

'They won't hurt a woman, that's what you mean.' Jesse leaned down to the candle and puffed his cigarette alight. 'This'll cost her all the same, and it's your doing.'

Calem dropped his head against his knees. A wave of remorseful misery swept him; his blind action had blundered them all into a trouble whose form he hadn't vaguely seen. Now as it took stark outline in his mind, he felt sick all over again,

'Hell,' Jesse said. 'It's done now. We ain't fixed to go on the dodge, so we'll sit tight and wait on Ma. She'll have grub and news. Then we'll ease out nice and quiet, if. If a lot of things.'

Calem muttered, 'You don't need to. I'll

43

make out,' aware that it qualified as a sulky little-boy statement.

'Shut up,' Jesse said thoughtfully, sighing out a streamer of smoke. 'We can't go west across the basin, Skull territory, which leaves north, south, east, and all points between.' He stretched out his legs, crossed them, and scowled at the wavering candle flame. 'Some rough travel north of here, desert and mountain, and damn little settlement. But Mercyville across the mountains has a strong police force, which could be useful in your case. How about it?'

'You asking me?'

There was ice in Jesse's grin. '*You're* on the dodge now, remember?'

Calem said nothing for a while, then shifted his back against the rock. 'Can they find this place?'

'Sooner or later. Look, kid, we can't stay here. Ma could fetch us grub, but sooner or later they'll put a lookout on the house so she can be followed. Take them a while to think of that, but sure as sunrise they will. Well. Make up your mind.'

Calem said numbly, 'North, then,' and stretched out on his side, hugging his arms. He let his breathing go lax and even, and pretended to sleep. He heard Jesse's shirt rasp on the rock as he stretched and yawned. He could almost feel that dark and sardonic gaze, and then Jesse said softly, 'You poor, sorry

44

bastard. You'll learn the rest of it soon enough . . .'

There was nothing to do but sleep and wait, and Calem found both almost impossible. He jerked fitfully awake at any slight sound, sweating, staring into total darkness—the candle having been snuffed against future need—while Jesse snored on. This was an old pattern for him, the lying low and the waiting, but Calem could only sprawl in nerve-strung wakefulness and stare into the dark and wrestle with the unavoidable question: how right had he been?

To a man raging against the wanton murder of his father, a natural retribution should seem clear-cut in its balancing of the scales, but even if he settled the rightness of the act to his mind, how did he write off the consequences? He had only to think of Ma to wish, in a wash of bitter remorse, that he could turn back the clock. But where was the right of seeing Pa's killer go free as the wind? If right could be wrong, black could be white, and Jesse, with his elemental guideline of cynical expediency, was closer to the reality of things. For Jesse, outside of his loyalty to mother and brother, the answer would be as clear-cut as another man's black and white. If your trouble was a small one, step on it; if a big one, run from it.

No, Calem thought stubbornly, you got to live by and for something. If there's no such thing as right or wrong, it can't stop a man worth his salt from living like there was. You got to start with that much, or nothing is worth anything.

Which answered no large questions, but eased his troubled mind with the thinking on it; the thought drifted, and he slept as dawn sent its first pale glow into the cave mouth.

*   *   *

He woke to a hand shaking him by the shoulder, and rolled over blinking against the dimness of the cave. 'Wake up, kid,' Jesse said. 'I been up three hours on the watch, and Ma's here.'

Calem scrambled through the tunnel. Bracing himself in the entrance, he heaved the saddlebags Jesse passed him onto the ledge above, and they aided one another's ascent to it. Martha Gault was waiting below, and within a minute they reached her side.

She murmured, 'My boys, my boys,' holding them both, and Calem realized with dismay that she was crying. He'd never seen that, even when Pa ... *but now it's all gone for her and your doing.* With the thought came a fresh pang of remorse. She had known hard times all her life, yet the part of living filled by Jared and her sons had been good, and now it was all gone.

She summoned her old briskness. 'Now, boys, have you decided on what's to be done?'

Jesse told her the plan, and she said worriedly, 'Do you know that country, Jess?'

'I can hold a line by the sun and stars, Ma, and three-four days should bring us over the mountains to Mercyville. I know it's due north of here, and the law there ain't owned by old Major Dembrow.'

'Good. I brought you blankets and grub.' She nodded toward the sack slung from the sidesaddle on the jughead roan standing nearby. 'Jerky and hardtack. You'll be making no fire, and you won't be disposed to no long stops. Hope you boys are appreciative of this. Been some long living since your ma rode that blamed rig.'

Jesse smiled. 'What-all since yesterday, Ma?'

She shook her head soberly. 'Nothing good. After you went after Calem I hitched up directly and drove to town. Heard about the shooting, learned what I could and got back home near nightfall. Old Man Dembrow was there, and his crew was going over the place. Didn't faze me, knowing Calem had got away and you boys 'ud meet on the road and come straight here. Got Pa's rifle and sent the lot packing. Set out for here this morning whilst it was still dark, case Dembrow had a man watching the place.'

'Good thinking,' Jesse said, and shook his head grimly. 'That old gimlet-eyed sidewinder. He'll never quit.'

'I reckon not,' Martha Gault said calmly. 'I don't excuse the man, but I know his feeling right enough. Ames was a rotten potato, but that's no never mind to a parent. Pinned his hopes on that boy, and he's lost him.'

That was for me, Calem thought miserably, and lowered his eyes.

Jesse said, 'Ma, you didn't raise any Skull men coming here?'

'I'd a turned back then,' she said tartly. 'No, but you bet they're out in force hunting the basin. Another thing, Dembrow's put old Abel Sutter on the scent, and that's bad.'

'Sutter? Is that old wolfer still batting around?'

'Last night he was with Dembrow, going over our place like a coon dog.'

'That's bad, right enough,' Jesse muttered.

The knowledge of old Abel Sutter dogging their trail was a cold breath on a man's spine. Sutter, the son of a mountain man and a Yaqui squaw, had developed the uncanny senses of the animals he had spent a lifetime trapping. Usually he kept to himself in the hills, now and then coming in to collect the scavenger bounty Major Dembrow paid, and to buy his meager needs: salt, tobacco, and rifle shells. It was said Abel Sutter could study a week-old track and tell you all except the critter's color, and this too if he could locate a hair or two. And Calem remembered when a neighbor's well went dry and how, after a dozen futile shafts

48

were sunk, Sutter was called in. He had simply pointed, 'Dig there,' and ten feet down water, plenty and pure, was found. 'Smelled it,' Sutter had said laconically. Or he might have analyzed details in the landscape, but nobody had questioned the explanation.

'Was hopeful,' Jesse said bleakly, 'we could start after dark and get clear of the basin without being picked up. Now, no point in waiting. Once that damn Injun cuts the sign we made yesterday or Ma's today, it's purely a matter of time, which we got none to lose.'

He headed for the notch where their horses were. Calem started to follow, but Martha said: 'Let Jess take care of things. Want you to hear good what I tell you now.'

'I—don't know what to say, Ma.'

'It's done,' Martha said matter-of-factly. 'Got to reckon with things as they are. No need your worrying for me. Plenty of kin in Missouri who'll see I don't lack, and I'm strong enough to hire out for my keep once I'm settled again. When you're free of this, you can join me there or not, up to you.'

'I will, Ma.'

She said sternly, 'Don't give your hasty word. A son's beholden only as there's a need, and I can make my way. You got a life to make for yourself.' She reached up a hand and smoothed back his unruly forelock, the gesture filled with a sadness and a compassion. 'My poor boy. You've chose a bitter way to get your

49

growth.'

'Was I wrong?'

'Man who killed your father should have hung, and you give him a chance he didn't deserve. No. I worried a spell about what it might do to you, was all.' She glanced toward Jesse as he led the horses from the notch to water, and lowered her voice. 'Watch out for him, Calem. Keep him with you as long as you can.'

He was openly surprised, and she said: 'Yes, he's the older, but in years only. Got myself little sleep last night, puzzling how it is with the two of you. You're the boy'll always make your own way, once you find your growth. It's Jesse needs something more, and he always will. Don't know as it was Jared's fault or a born lack in the boy. I'm inclined to think both, and I can't see the end of it, but I'm afraid. Try to keep him with you, Calem.'

'I will,' he began, then amended humbly that he would try.

They filled their saddlebags to bulging with most of the stores Martha had packed, caching the rest in their blanket-rolls. She had brought Jared's rifle and saddle scabbard too, his old canteen, and all the cartridges she could find for Calem.

'We'll backtrack out of these hills,' Jesse said brusquely, 'then swing north along the edge of the basin. Ma, you ride out ahead of us till we're clear of the brush. Give a holler if you see anything. No telling but they're close on this place already, and we'll have to run for it.'

'Take care, boys.' She held Jesse a moment, then Calem, and she was close to breaking again. Jesse assisted her to mount, and she put the jughead across the clearing and was lost to sight in the trees.

'All right, kid. I'll lead out, and we'll go easy.'

Mounting, they moved into the trees along the game trail. Calem sat bolt upright, his reins moist against his palm, while Jesse rocked to his horse's gait at a careless slouch. It might have been a game to him, except for the restlessness of his eyes conning the sun-mottled glades. Presently, the trees thinned away; they climbed to high and rocky ground where deep brush flourished, well-broken by the trail. As the brush too gave way to open country, they caught an occasional glimpse of Martha, always keeping a good hundred yards to her back.

Calem's breathing eased when he saw the first rolling sage flats of the east basin, and as they came down the last slope, Jesse halted and raised in his stirrups and waved his hand. Martha responded, and Calem lifted his hand and let it slowly settle to his pommel, and his throat tightened up. He did not look again as Jesse quartered off along the slope, northward now.

51

They rode for a steady hour, and as the terrain roughened once more, found themselves close to Horseshoe Gap, a deep irregular pass that cut through the north basin ramparts. It would take them into the Arrowhead Breaks, a lonely and sterile region of sun-blasted rock that marked the atrophied spine of an ancient mountain range.

Hard by the gap, Jesse swung offtrail and skirted a ridge that thrust up like a knotty gray fist. Its far side mellowed into a gradual incline, and here he left the saddle. He said, 'We'll have a look from above,' and taking a pair of Army fieldglasses from his saddlebag, swung up the ridge like a mountain goat. Calem followed more slowly, panting and sweat-drenched when he achieved the summit, and threw himself down by Jesse. They were belly-prone on a shelving ledge over a steep drop. Jesse braced his elbows and trained his glasses on the hilly sweep of a rock-studded flat they had crossed.

Calem saw his shoulders stiffen. 'What is it?'

'Something I saw move. And there again, by God. A horse-backer, sure enough.'

'How many?'

'Just the one, I think. Wait a while.'

The rider was hard to make out on the neutral slope, but straining along Jesse's line of sight, Calem shortly saw him move across the brow of a hill. 'He getting down?'

'Yeah,' Jesse said bitterly. 'Him all right,

Sutter. Knew he'd cut our sign somewhere, but I never figured he would breathe down our necks this soon. Would reckon he'll make sure we're pointed north through the gap, then ride to fetch the Major and his boys.'

Jesse edged back off the rim on his hands and belly so as not to skyline himself, and then pulled half-erect. He handed Calem the glasses. 'Wait here and keep flattened down. Keep them glasses steady so's you won't catch the sun.'

Calem opened his mouth, but Jesse was already gone, scrambling down the ridgeflank. Calem raised to his elbows and sighted in the glasses. In a moment he caught the old wolfer in the act of mounting up after checking the ground.

Sutter was a small man, desiccated and weather-stained by years of desert sun and wind. His greasy elkhide leggins were worn smoothly black, and his oft-patched calico shirt was threadbare and faded. His face was flat and gaunt and scarred, the muscles of it so prominent that it resembled a flayed mask, except for the stirring of his gray-whiskered jaw on a tobacco cud. His eyes, even in the shadow of his battered hat, were as blue and clear-cold as pond ice. Sutter rode toes out, heels gently flailing, like the Apaches he had once tracked for the Army.

Jesse's boots scraped softly to his re-ascent, and bellying down and inching up by Calem

53

again, he found a bracing rock for his rifle.

'Jess?'

Calem's voice sounded shrill to his own ears, and Jesse said with a peculiar flatness: 'He'll get us killed if he stays onto us. I don't aim to wait on him. Won't get another chance like this. Shut your mouth and don't bat an eye.'

He took the glasses from Calem, sighting again. Calem's heart triphammered against the rock while the slow seconds dragged into minutes. Sutter, not dismounting again, rode slowly and saddle-bent to scan the ground. He was within easy sighting now, and Jesse's rifle barrel ground gently on the rock as he aimed. Then his sweating cheek left the rifle stock; he swore irritably. Abel Sutter had reined up, his head tilting erect, and horse and man became motionless as statues.

Couldn't have seen us, Calem thought, and then remembering old Jourgenson's well, felt his spine crawl even as his mind rejected the thought. As slight a thing as a telltale flick of his pony's ears, for the animal and man were like one, might have alerted Sutter. Something for sure, since he reined his mount sideways to turn back.

Jesse fired, as the horse came around full-flank to his sights. The paint went down, its forequarters smashed by the long rifle slug, and Sutter, yanking his rifle from its boot, twisted free of the stirrups. He balled his body

54

and hit the stony ground rolling. Almost before he was on his feet, as the clap of shot echoes died off, he was lunging away. Jesse shot again, dusting the wolfer with powdery splinters from a flat boulder as he dived behind it.

'Most I hoped for at this range was to put him afoot,' Jesse observed as a rifle spoke by the flat boulder. The paint horse had been thrashing in the rocks, and its struggles ceased. 'Well, that old horse meant a lot to him. It is hell or high water for us now, far as he's concerned. Meantime he is laid up good in a stand-off, and he can outlast us. Seeing we've earned us a little time, let's get down off of this and ride.'

CHAPTER FIVE

They left the breaks the next day, after crossing shattered ridges, pushing through tortuous arroyos, and leading their mounts down or up treacherous slides of rock. The third dawn found them climbing the fairly regular upgrade formed by an arching saddle between several peaks. Jesse called a halt, after a rough climb to the highest dip of the saddle.

Calem was glad to step down and hold the drooping, lathered horses while Jesse ascended to a flinty spur and trained his fieldglasses on their backtrail. When he had clambered down, his face was grim. 'I counted six. They made good time. Old Sutter likely knows this country like the lines of his hand. Followed the good trails while we felt our way through and run ourselves up box canyons.'

Calem said in a parched croak, 'How far behind?'

'Three hours, or four.' Jesse wrapped the strap around his field glasses and jammed them in his saddlebag. He uncapped his canteen, rolled some water in his mouth and swallowed it. 'Sooner or later they will sure-hell overhaul us, and I'd a sight rather it was after we reach yonder peaks.' He added, 'If we got to stand and fight, good cover will narrow the odds,' in a tone indicating that the odds would still be bad.

Calem surveyed the far sweep of mountains to the north, darkened baseward by a cling of heavy timber, soaring into snow-veined pinnacles. These were the peaks of his grandfather's lusty times; there was no thrill in their proximity. The ruthless pace Jesse had set had etched a strained exhaustion into every fiber of Calem's body, and his nerves screamed for rest. He looked at Jesse, whose grimy face was a gaunt, alkaline mask relieved only by a black smudge of beard and the slitted paleness of his eyes. Calem ran a tongue over his cracked lips, knowing he looked no better. His mouth was gritty, and his eyeballs grated in their sockets; he felt as if the tissues of his body were sucked clean.

Between them and the first green foothills lay a scorched and naked arm of rock-broken desert. Though they had conserved their water, one third-canteenful was all that remained to carry them to the first water, wherever it might be. Hard pursued, they dared not lay up till night relieved the heat which laid its flat dead hand on a man's body and mind.

Jesse soaked a corner of his bandanna from his canteen and swabbed out the caked dust from his horse's nostrils. Calem did the same, and took a smooth pebble from his pocket and stuck it in his mouth, nursing it for a ghost of moisture. He said: 'Jesse—we best state it plain. Water is the big problem.'

'Sure.' Bleakly Jesse shook his canteen. 'Never make it on what's left between us, but I'm gambling we'll hit water before ...'

When he did not finish, Calem put in, 'We had sure ought to. Why, Jess, there's always watering places if a body knows 'em.'

'Sure, sure,' Jesse said irritably. 'Might be one right under our feet, eh? Wager that damned Sutter knows every water clear to the mountains, and if so, it's more edge for them. Nothing for it, and we ain't buying any time here.'

They took their plodding way down the far

side of the saddle-shaped pass, and by noon left it for the barren country below. It was a cruel and heat-blasted desolation, laced by catclaw and mesquite and more kinds of cacti than Calem had ever seen. Stretches of baked, crack-seamed flats were interspersed by scattered reaches of jagged, clustered rocks that formed weird, monolithic shapes against the sky and threw grotesque shadows with the deepening afternoon.

Bringing up the rear, Calem found himself looking back repeatedly, straining his eyes for a sign of the pursuers. In the past two days he had learned about the nerve-strung state of a hunted man: a haunting and gut-deep fear that blotted out a man's character and convictions with a terrifying ease. Jesse had lived with it before this, and yesterday Jesse would have killed Abel Sutter without warning, without a second thought. *And I would of let him.*

The knowledge brought home to Calem his naked and vulnerable ignorance of life, of himself. Was becoming case-hardened against all better feelings the real key to survival? He thought doggedly that this was Jesse's way, not his, as even Jess had admitted: *You ain't cut from the same cloth as me, kid ... you don't know the half of it.* But he was learning fast, and he wondered whether in spite of everything Jesse's price for naked survival could become his own. Already he had let plain fear and not a moral measure of the act against the stakes govern him; how many times could a man forswear his moral qualms and his deepest nature go unchanged?

The afternoon was far gone, the flat sunslant painting the rocks dull orange and making deep maroon shadows, when a wink of pale green foliage ahead caught Calem's eye. The buckskin pricked up his ears at the prospect of water, and followed the bay as Jesse kicked into a lope. They crossed a low ridge and dipped onto its far side. Below was a shallow seep rimmed by a greenery of willow and scrub cottonwood. Calem reined up and piled out of his saddle in a hurry, and Jesse said sharply, 'You hold on. I'll try it.' He came off his saddle, moved stiff-legged to the edge of the seep and stretched out on his belly. He dipped up a double handful of water and tasted it; his face screwed into a wry grimace and he spat. 'Minerals. Might be sound water could a man gag it down, but first it would bind up his jaw. Hell!'

He rocked back on his heels, and picked up a twig and twirled it between his fingers. 'The gamble was that we find water soon. Well, this is it, and it's no good.' He paused to isolate his next words. 'The way I see it, we got one chance. It's pushing a hard pace while the sun dries you out that uses up water, and we won't last another day on what we got. We had best keep on the move tonight and lay up tomorrow first sun. Tomorrow midnight should see us deep in the mountains. Be water aplenty then. Will mean a long while getting there, but at least we will.'

Calem stared at him. 'Jess, you said yourself they're three, four hours behind us, and likely they have cut it to one or two by now. If Sutter knows of good water, they're in a sight the better shape, not to say their horses. They'll overhaul us in short order, then—'

'With horses,' Jesse cut in softly.

'Sure with horses.'

Without another word Jesse rose and stalked to his black; he stepped into the saddle and reined around and kicked into a lunging climb of the ridge they had just crossed.

'Jesse!'

'I ain't crazy, Cal. Come along and I'll tell you while we ride.' He dropped downridge in the direction from which they had come. Swearing under his breath, Calem caught up his reins, mounted, and swung after him.

While they rode and Jesse talked, the light faded swiftly from the land, and only its memory welted the far sky like a vast bloodstain. The rocky scape took on a muted purpling, and its harsh outlines lost substance in the thickening dusk. The desert became alive with small sounds, strange rustlings of brush and a coyote's bay and the hoot of a great horned owl coasting on silent wing as it scanned for prey. Finally, some two hundred yards to the south of them, Calem saw the orange glimmer of a fire.

This was as near as they could get on horseback without alerting the camp. They dropped off their mounts and settled on their hunkers, and waited for the camp to sleep. Jesse was counting on the relaxed vigilance of Dembrow and his men. For his quarry to backtrack and counterstrike should be so unexpected that even an ex-military man might easily forego the field habit of posting a night guard. The audacity of the plan and its element of surprise were the best augurs for success; otherwise it seemed so foolhardy that sickly tension had left Calem hollow-bellied long before they spotted the fire.

After what seemed a young eternity Jesse said meagerly, 'Time to move,' and came to his feet heel-grinding a cigarette he had rolled and not lighted. On foot leading the horses they moved in, carefully avoiding rocks. The moon's silvery disc was half-full tonight, bathing out tortured contours of rock, making pale and ghostly exposure where it touched and fathomless shadow where it did not. But Dembrow's men within the rim of firelight would be nearly blind, looking toward the outer darkness.

Presently Jesse raised his hand for a halt. They were near enough to make out a half-dozen blanketed forms around the fire, its light caught on the murky glint of a spring to which Abel Sutter's lore had guided them.

There was a plot of grass and scrub timber, and a horse picket line was stretched between two treeboles.

Jesse motioned with his finger, making a half-circle which indicated they would sweep wide and get south of the camp, enabling them to push the horses north. They moved forward again, this time halting a scant twenty yards beyond the firelight. Jesse passed Calem his reins and sat down, and worked off his boots. Afterward he went on alone, ducking noiselessly from rock to rock, then going down on his belly and crawling the remaining distance.

Abruptly a man came bolt upright in his blankets. Calem waited, holding his breath. The man was Abel Sutter of course, but what had alerted him? Then Calem realized how the horses had ceased their usual restless noises. They had heard Jesse or caught his scent; for Sutter this single break in the night's pattern was enough.

Jesse had melted into the ground shadows, and belly-flat and motionless he was as good as invisible. Sutter was on his feet now, rifle in hand; he glided warily off from the fire. *He can't be sure without he can see in the dark.* Calem's spine tingled; a man could be sure of nothing where Abel Sutter was concerned. The old wolfer sank to his haunches just beyond the firelight, his faint outline an aching blur in Calem's eyes.

It seemed a long while after the horses had resumed their normal stirrings that Sutter rose and paced back to his blankets, evidently concluding that a scavenger had disturbed them and passed on. Calem lost track of time waiting for Jesse's next move which did not come till Sutter had apparently relaxed in sleep. Now Jesse slithered with infinite care to the nearest tree securing the picket rope. Without raising his body he thrust a quick-flashing knife between knot and bark. Twisting on his belly, he inched back the way he had come.

The freed horses increased their restive stirrings, again rousing Abel Sutter, this time at once. He came to his feet in a turning motion that shed his blankets; he cocked his rifle as his eyes swept the night.

Again Jesse froze in position, and for a coldly uncertain moment, Calem's hand tensed around his gunbutt. Sutter would fire at the first hint of sound, and Calem knew that to give Jesse a chance he might have to kill the wolfer. But he had underbid Jesse's resources; suddenly Jesse half-lifted himself and let go with the blood-chilling shriek of a cougar.

Instant panic rushed over the standing horses. Starting to bolt, they entangled themselves in the severed rope but only momentarily; the end horse slipped free and the others followed one by one, thundering away into the night.

Sutter had whipped up his rifle at once, pumping shots at the source of the shriek, but now he wheeled at a stiff lope after the escaping horses. Jesse was on his feet now, coming toward Calem in a sidling half-run, at the same time opening up with his pistol, trying for Sutter while the chance offered itself. But Sutter was already swallowed by the darkness, and cursing, Jesse sprinted to Calem's side and snatched his reins and vaulted into saddle. 'Come on—come on!'

He put his horse in a heedless run after the stampeding remuda. Calem's fleeting glimpse of the camp as they passed showed it in utter pandemonium. He had a vivid impression of Jeffrey Dembrow in the firelight, his white hair awry, his stocky legs planted apart.

Moments later came his crisply barked orders; a spattering of gunfire broke out behind them, and Calem thought, *They can't see us but they hear us right enough.* He bent low to the buckskin's mane, and then a rifle spoke off to their left. He saw the wink of muzzleflash and heard Jesse shout and return fire. That would be Sutter, and he knew from the drift of pounding hoofs ahead that the entire remuda had eluded the wolfer and he was turning on the marauders. These things made chaotic splinters of sensation and thought, and then all of it, the camp and Sutter and the sporadic crackle of gunfire, was behind them. There was only the rake of brush

64

along his legs and the cool rush of air along his clammy face. They were on an open flat flooded by rock-fretted moonlight and ahead of them raced the Dembrow remuda, a silver haze of dust bannering up behind it.

Jesse shouted, 'Hyah, hyah,' and pulled flank-on to the animals, crowding them toward a rambling wall of cliff. He meant to box the herd, Calem realized, and came abreast of the remuda on its other side. They pointed the horses into a shallow cleft indenting the base of the tortured scarp and successfully milled them to a blowing, lathered standstill.

Calem sidled the buckskin back and forth to keep the animals confined, thinking that Jesse had been right: one daring blow had broken the pursuit; now they had only to drive the horses ahead of them a ways, then turn them loose. It would be dawn before Abel Sutter could start tracking them down, and by the time they came on the horses, Jess and he would have a safe margin of many hours on them.

Turning to his brother, he saw with horror that Jesse had folded across his pommel, both hands gripping his left thigh above the knee. A dark spreading stain soaked his pantsleg, and when Calem's voice pulled his glance, the moon on his face showed the drawn tightness of shock and pain.

Calem made a move to step down, but savagely Jesse shook his head. 'Never mind.

Hold them horses.' He paused, drawing deep, shuddering breaths as he mustered effort, then heaved a leg free of stirrup and stepped carefully to the ground. He eased himself onto his buttocks, grunting, and pulled his knife. Grasping his thigh tight above the wound, he slit his trouser leg.

Calem said numbly, 'Sutter?'

'I reckon. Only one not shooting blind, wasn't he?' He felt gingerly around to the back of his leg. 'So I'm lucky for a change and she went clean through. Old lead in a man's gizzard acts up now and then.'

The wound was deep enough, but did not appear otherwise serious, the bullet having taken him through the big muscle slightly front and well to the side of the bone. Yet it could prove a fatal blow to the advantage they had seized. The injury would slow their pace and take its savage, inevitable toll of Jesse's strength. Jesse said between his teeth, 'Dig out that sack of flour and that clean spare shirt of yours, and toss them down here.'

Calem did so, without leaving his saddle. Jesse dug into the flour, plastering great handfuls of its cool whiteness over both openings of his wound, and it caked the blood at once. 'Will help some, though I'll leak plenty more if we're long in the saddle and no help for it.' He tore the shirt into strips for compresses, knotting them into place around his thigh. He stuffed the flapping trouser leg into his boot and taking up his reins, inched to his feet. He took hold of the stirrup and worked the foot of his sound leg into it and heaved himself across the saddle, grunting with the agony of effort. For a moment he was bowed over with pain, then his voice came curt and crisp:

'All right, let's haze them out.'

They loose-herded the remuda north along the base of the scarp, Calem keeping a worried eye on Jesse. For a time he held erect, rocking precisely to his horse's gait. Calem watched for the dull slackness to take him, then reined over to him and took hold of his reins, saying, 'Let go,' and when Jesse obeyed, 'You're about done. We got to lay up.'

Jesse roused himself with a sighing effort. 'Not on my account. Ride on if you want.'

'Shut up, Jess. No more talk like that.'

'They ain't wanting me.'

His face was polished with sweat, and his breathing carried a husky note; he was plainly in no shape to go on. Calem's own body ached for sleep, and his eyeballs burned in their parched sockets. Dembrow and his party, stranded afoot, would not be coming up fast, and for both of them a few hours' rest was a grim necessity.

Ahead he saw a sparsely grassed bench with a rim of moon-whitened boulders. Here was a natural breastworks, and a little graze for the horses. Calem pulled up beyond the boulders and swung stiffly down. Jesse had started to cant sideways in the saddle, and Calem caught his slack weight and eased him to the ground. Then he threw the rigs off the horses and hobbled them on the grass under the trees. He spread his brother's ground blanket and laid him on it and spread his own tarp and blankets above him. Jesse's teeth were chattering, and he would be burning up with fever soon, Calem knew. All he could do was keep him warm and give him some of their precious water. Shaking out his coiled rope, he folded its length twice and started for the Dembrow horses standing tiredly nearby. He broke into a run, swinging the doubled rope, and with hoarse cries hoorawed the animals to a run, scattering them.

Afterward he settled himself in the rocks, his rifle tucked in his folded arms, but sleep was slow coming in spite of his exhaustion. The whole situation, the judgments and actions to take, was transferred suddenly to his shoulders, gripping him with an uneasy strangeness. By the time he was growing drowsy, Jesse groaned for water and he roused himself to fetch it.

He passed the night that way, occasionally breaking a dozing vigil to tend Jesse as he sank into fever and delirium. Most of it was incoherent babbling, but a few words came through concerning a girl named Florie, and once he called, 'Ma,' with a lost, wrenching note. Recalling Martha's words—'Jesse needs something more'—Calem wondered what was Jesse's real need if his hardened self-sufficiency were a mask. Maybe for some men there was no answer. When you came down to it, the only thing on which all men agreed was the need for survival . . .

With that thought, he found himself toying on the idea of taking Jesse's advice, leaving him and pushing on alone. Yet the unwritten law of the country, to give help when it was needed, might be written off in Major Dembrow's present temper. He and the men with him knew Jesse from years ago, and they knew the reputation he had garnered since. Even if the Major's personal fury did not extend to Jesse, there was reason to suppose that the pursuit party, coming on him, would simply leave him to die. And Calem discarded the notion with no doubts.

CHAPTER SIX

At the pearly light of first dawn, he breakfasted off a handful of jerked beef and a meager swallow of water, and prepared for the trail. Jesse was feverish but sluggishly rational as Calem changed the blood-soaked bandages, using another shirt for the job. He hoisted Jesse into the saddle and, taking no chances,

69

lashed his wrists to the horn and secured his ankles by running a rope under the horse's barrel.

Losing no time, he mounted and led out, threading the rocky upheaval of the desert floor. By now the gently rounded foothills below the saw-toothed range to the north seemed tantalizingly near, but at this snail's pace it was still most of a day's travel to them. His frequent, worried backglances at Jesse showed his head rolling slackly on his chest, and it came to him that even this idle, jogging pace could start the wound bleeding afresh.

Soon Jesse's sagging form was hunched deeply over his pommel, and when Calem said his name, there was no response. He halted and fell back by his brother's stirrup, feeling a dismal nudge of fear. Jesse's eyes were glazed over, and his whole trouser leg was soaked with blood. Calem kneaded his sun-cracked lower lip between his teeth, staring across their backtrail, hesitating. The sun was starting its slow climb, and a new day's heat already simmered in the air. Calem lifted his canteen and shook it, and then scanning about, saw a squat *bisnaga* cactus growing between two rocks.

In Jesse's condition a day in the saddle would probably finish him, but to lay up now would whittle precious hours from the delay last night's coup had provided. Yet there was no choice, and he felt a leaden thrust of despair. No use deluding himself that Jesse could survive long in these circumstances; he needed more than what ignorant care Calem could give, and they were unknown miles from any habitation.

Then he heard the rifle shot.

Its ringing, not-distant crack brought him motionless, disbelieving, listening to a pulse of echoes die away. Dembrow? Not this close and not this soon.

He reined the horses over to an outcrop spur of rock; he stepped down and untied Jesse, easing him to the ground. He threw off gear and spread ground tarps and blankets in the warm scanty shade, and made Jesse as comfortable as possible.

He climbed atop the spur and shaded his eyes against the blaze of a young raw day. If there were an army out in that desolation, the waste of jumbled rock could have concealed it. The teeming life of desert night had withdrawn, and all was unstirring silence now. Once he saw a chuckwalla skitter beneath a rock, and a carrion bird sailed lazily along the high currents.

Calem's spine crawled strangely, and he thought, *Now it's nerves,* and came down off the spur as Jesse gave a faint, heaving groan. It sounded like 'Water,' but there was no recognition in his glazed stare. Calem lifted his head, tilted the canteen to his lips and this time let him finish the water. Then carrying

71

both canteens he moved over to the *bisnaga*, settled on his hunkers and plunged his knife into it near the crown. Careful to avoid the barbed spines that would work into the living flesh they hooked, he carved a ring-shaped cut around the barrel cactus and pried off its top.

He filled his hands with wet pulp, made hard fists and squeezed it out drop by drop into the canteens. After long aching hours of this he would have a small supply of something qualifying as liquid. He dully wondered if it mattered now, but it was something to occupy his attention while waiting for Major Dembrow . . .

Squatting thus, he dozed on the thought, his hands relaxing. The sound of grating rock snatched him to alertness. A shadow falling across the cactus yanked him around, pivoting on his heels.

'Don't start up like that again, mister,' the boy said, 'or I'll blow you clean apart before you bat a winker.'

The sun was in Calem's eyes, and it took him a confused instant to realize the boy must have come up unseen on the far side of the outcrop. He stood slight and stiff atop the rotted abutment, a Winchester long rifle tucked against his side.

Calem blinked to focus, only then realizing that the sun and the boyish brusqueness of the young voice had deceived him. This was a girl, not much past twelve, he thought, almost lost in a patched and oversize duck jacket and slouch hat. Her eyes were blue and fierce and solemn in a thin, sun-darkened face; she held the rifle with a negligent competence that warned him to make no move.

She said quietly, 'You just stand so,' and descended the spur as nimbly as a ground squirrel. 'Now,' she motioned with the rifle, 'you set a saddle on that buckskin and be quick about it.'

Calem found his voice. 'You aim to steal a horse?'

She said flatly, 'I need him,' as if it explained everything. 'You do like I say.'

Calem stiffened his shoulders in the odd, dogged manner of his father. 'I don't reckon I will.'

'But I do.' Her eyes narrowed, making faint sun-wrinkles at their corners; she cocked the rifle. 'Boy, you move now.'

Calem measured the distance between them with his eyes and knew she could drop him before he covered half of it. From the look of her, probably she would, too. But a wild stubbornness was in him now; he had been goaded too far and too long, and with no doubts at all he hunched his head and started toward her.

The rifle roared, almost in his face it seemed; he felt a sharp tug at his hat. He halted, not looking at the fallen hat, letting his stare lock the girl's in a wordless clash.

'Go on.'

'I will! You better believe that!' Savagely she cocked the rifle again, and he wondered if the tremor in her unyielding voice were fury or desperation. 'Next time I will!'

Calem hauled a deep breath and started walking again. Three yards from her, he saw the rage and protest rise in her face and knew that if his refusal to obey did not crowd her to decision, panic might. She began, 'I warned—' and not waiting then, he drove his toes against the earth, pistoning his legs, and came into her in a low lunge, grappling her around the waist. The rifle exploded above his head, and the barrel came down in a slashing arc across his back, wrenching a painful grunt from him as they fell together.

She was wiry as a colt, and for twenty furious seconds he had his hands full as she tried to brain him with the rifle, then with a rock, sputtering, 'Goddam you, I'll kill you!' He did not want to hurt her, but he nearly yielded to impulse before he straddled her on his knees, pinning her wrists against the small of her back. After a writhing moment she relaxed with a panting sigh, twisting up a dirtsmudged face. 'Let up, boy. Let me up now.'

There was pure venom in her look, and he grunted, 'Not much, without you stay quiet.'

'All right.'

Holding her wrists one-handed he picked up

74

her rifle and only then released her. She retrieved her hat, lost in the scuffle, and came to her feet beating the dust from it. Her unevenly cropped hair was cut short in a boy's crude waterfall, and she glared through the pale, sun-bleached tangle of it, then tossed it back. She was well over twelve, he realized now, though her generous mouth and pugnose enhanced a childlike quality. But like many girl-women of a small, sturdy build she carried a surprising fullness at hip and bosom, this not at once apparent in her shapeless duck jacket and dress. The skirt was fairly short, coming to just below the knee; though her high deerhide leggin-moccasins covered her decently enough, it was a curiosity to see a white girl dressed so.

'Suppose you say why you want that horse so all-fire bad?'

'None of your damn business.' Her nostrils flared faintly, and clamping on the hat then, she glanced abruptly at Jesse. 'What's wrong with him?'

'Shot. Look, miss—'

'I'm Charley Jacks. That's to say Charlotte Lee Jacks.' She made a wry grimace. 'I make it Charley; you too, y'hear?' She shuttled her bird-quick glance from Jesse's face back to his. 'He your brother?'

Calem nodded wearily. 'I'm Calem Gault, he's Jesse. Listen—'

'My pa could fix him up right enough.'

That gave a sharp tug to his fine-crowded

75

hopes. 'Your pa. Is he far away?'

'A few miles.' She tilted her head vaguely toward the southeast; she set her fists on hips, a small frown touching her brow. 'Mister, I surely need that horse. Reckon we could dicker about it?'

'Maybe,' Calem said cautiously. Meeting anyone at all in this Godforsaken waste was unexpected enough; meeting a strange, mercurial waif of a girl like this one was downright baffling. Probably she was someone's nameless woods colt; no proper father would let his lawful daughter run out of harness so, and she could use a halter on that evil tongue. 'Maybe, if your pa knows doctoring, we could make a deal. My brother needs looking to, and soon.'

She laughed shortly. 'You ain't asking much.'

Calem stared at her a dismal and weary moment, thinking that there was an idiotic quality to this talk, and indeed to the whole situation. He supposed being tense and nerve-frayed lent reality a nightmarish hue; he couldn't shake the feeling that he might awake at any moment in his own bed at home. He blinked, mustering himself for the effort of speech. 'How's that?'

'My pa needs help for himself, that's how. Why I need your horse. You hear a shot a while back? Me. Had to kill the horse. Rode him too hard and busted a leg for him, which

76

was a fool thing. We got no other.'

'We was talking,' Calem said a little unsteadily, 'about your pa.'

Miss Charley Jacks fingered a long scratch on her cheek; she looked off toward the broken heights southeast, and while she talked on, he caught the shades of emotion that colored her voice. They were not easy to pick out of the peculiar flatness of her tone. As she told it, she and her father lived alone; they owned and worked a gold diggings, and yesterday her father was in the tunnel when a shoring timber collapsed. His leg was pinioned, and after a night of wrestling with debris, she was unable to free him. This morning she had saddled their one horse and started for Mercyville. It lay a good day's ride beyond a saddle of peaks, but it was the only place to find help. Only her haste had crippled the bay, and shortly after shooting it and pushing on afoot, she'd spotted their horses in the lee of this rock and had stolen up to take them unawares.

Calem eyed her wonderingly. 'Didn't it occur to you to ask for help instead of throwing down on us?'

'What kind of ninny you take me for, mister? My pa is pinned by a big timber which is holding up a lot of loose rock. I cleared away part of the rock, but did not dast dig more for fear of bringing down the whole shebang and burying him. Only way to free him without

77

moving more rock is to raise the timber and the rock with it. I couldn't budge it, but might be three-four men could.' Her light, appraising stare held a quiet contempt. 'Mister, one man and his stove-up brother ain't no use to me.'

'Be that as it may,' Calem said grimly. 'You want my horse and I'm in a position to name terms. You ain't.'

She considered for a moment, then shrugged. 'Well, then.'

'Can't give my brother decent care out here. You lead me to shelter and a bed for him, and the horse is yours. Loan of it, I mean. I'll stay by Jess and see to your pa's needs too, till you get back with them Mercyville fellows.' He hesitated. 'Does he really know doctoring?'

'Pa? Said so, didn't I? Say, how 'bout my rifle?'

'I like to got brained with it once—'

Again her nostrils flared. 'We made a deal. Boy, that better come to more meaning than talk, or you can keep your damn horse and the whole kiboodle and choke on it.'

Calem nodded once, resignedly, and handed the rifle to her. Charley Jacks favored him with a stiff glare, but then gave a ready and willing hand as he set to packing the gear, and helped him tie Jesse in saddle again.

On foot, they set out southeast by the sun. The buckskin was still strong and brisk-stepping, yet showed the slow wear of the grueling trek. If he kept his promise to the girl, her streak of impetuous temper and the urgency of her need might mean the buckskin would share her horse's fate; she would not spare it on the sixty-mile-or-so ride to Mercyville, and that worried him. Even now, not trusting her with the buckskin's reins, he let her lead the bay with Jesse lashed to the saddle. She walked beside him at a free, tireless stride for all her diminutive size. And presently she remarked: 'What you-all running from?'

Calem gave her a wary, startled glance, and she said dryly, 'Maybe your brother done the job on himself, huh? Or you did?'

Calem's instinct was to dissemble, but she had guessed this much rightly. 'Some men following us. Looking to nail my hide, not his, but it went the other way.'

The girl stopped in her tracks. 'Listen. Pull up.' He did, and then she said flatly, 'Suppose you say what kind of a jackpot you have come from? Maybe we want no mix with it.'

Her frank eyes were like blued gunsteel, and he shifted uncomfortably. 'I killed this man's son—'

'What I want to know, was he looking at you when you fetched him?'

'Square in the eye.'

'That's all right, but—' Her small frown held, and she slightly tilted her head. 'They on your trail? Close by?'

'We lost 'em a good ways back yesterday.'

As they moved on then, Calem felt a tinge of shame for the lie, and uneasily now, he wondered if there were some bitter significance in his sudden glibness. A few short days ago he would have stammered and flushed over an untruth. For all, it seemed, that a man's conscience could sway against fear and desperation, these had a way of battering aside scruple and will. And desperate for help, afraid of her rebuff, if she were aware that his enemies would be close on his trail shortly, he was willing to more than lie, Calem knew. *It's for Jess, and not like the choice was so all-fire personal.*

CHAPTER SEVEN

During the last leg of their flight, he and Jesse had held wherever possible to the flatter and lower country. Now the girl was leading him in a deliberate way toward higher ground. Ahead lay a long, wavering line of vaulting, canyon-broken ridges, which in fact he had widely skirted earlier. As the terrain roughened, the climbing sun flooded it with a broiling fury; waves of mind-dulling heat danced off every tilting rock surface. Toiling up the first rocky ascent, Calem felt his lungs start to labor; his vision grew spotty and aching.

Miss Charley Jacks bounced up the

precipitous lift of a massive scarp like a nimble goat; now and then she had an ingenuous curse for the bay because it stumbled or shied. Calem was about to warn her against the reckless pace when, slowing of her own accord, she led the way onto a narrow ribbon of ledge. He saw that it was actually a trail that angled in a mounting terrace along the sheer upper wall of this cone-shaped formation, following its slow curve out of sight. It looked like a deep natural fault in the scarp, but here and there were signs of chipping and flaking, the work of primitive long-dead hands.

Miss Charley moved carefully now, speaking softly to the bay, feeling out its every step with her own. The rimrock was notched with gaps where huge chunks of crumbling scale had sloughed away into a sheer drop of hundreds of feet. As they climbed around the steep-mounting curve, the trail narrowed steadily till an unreasoning fear touched him that it would pinch off altogether, boxing and stranding them on this high, cramped shelf. Their horses' right stirrups scraped along the wall, dislodging pebbles that trickled over the rim. Clammy sweat distilled on his belly and back as he put his whole attention to negotiating past a bulging shoulder of cliff, and then a thin sigh left him. The trail widened out just ahead, and the crowding wall itself tapered off in a gentle grade that formed the far side of the conical ridge.

Now they were within the pocketing heights, and the slope below plunged gently away to a small valley half overgrown by a surprising luxuriance of scrub timber, accounted for by a stream which wound like a sparkling snake under the soft green of fringing willows.

Miss Charley Jacks said, 'There it is.'

'Where?' He saw no cabin or sheds, and the trees were too low and sparse to conceal a layout.

She said flatly, 'Look high, jughead,' and without more ado led off on the faint trace of the old trail as it continued downslope. Calem hesitated, sweeping his glance across the dipping basin. This terminated on its east side in a long incline running straight up to the base of a bare flinty ridge that rose sheer for a good thirty feet to a thrusting bulge of rimrock. Beyond that, apparently, lay only the brassy sky and a monotonous series of more dun-colored ridges.

Mystified, he followed the girl down to the valley where they angled through the timber, crossed the stream at a shallow fording, and came to the valley's east end. A clear spring that was the source of the stream bubbled from the rocks there, and Calem's throat constricted with a violent sudden thirst. But the girl, not pausing, tackled the long boulder-strewn incline. It was laced with smaller rubble that cascaded away in small chuckling slides.

A long sore ache was settling into his legs as

they neared the base of the ridge where the slope had its terminus. And abruptly then, he understood. The dwelling, almost invisible from beyond a few yards, was literally a part of the ridge-flank. Wind and weather had scored a large, horizontal niche into the softer rock that formed the lower ridge. A single curving wall that made a rusty blend with the rock had been built across the niche to form a room; and Calem recognized it as the work of Indian hands. He'd seen such cliffside structures before, with their half-round facing walls of small stones mortared together by a strange red cement even harder than the stones. Prehistoric men had built them as vaults for the dead and sealed them off. But this one had been built for the living; a narrow wooden doorframe was set in the rocks, its puncheon door hung by rawhide hinges and camouflaged by a red stain the hue of the rocks.

'Canyon back of the ridge has plenty grass and water,' Miss Charley told him. 'We kept the horse there. Best your animals be cooled off and watered and get a rest. I'll take 'em to the canyon and tend them while you fetch your brother inside.' She held out her hand and, after a moment's hesitation, Calem surrendered the reins. He unsecured the ropes and eased Jesse into his arms, and while Miss Charley removed the saddles and other gear, carried him inside.

The single room was surprisingly spacious,

with the sides of the niche forming the floor and ceiling and back wall. Two small windows, hardly more than wood-framed portholes with wooden shutters, flanked the door. The shutters were flung wide to admit dusty sunshafts that partly relieved a dim gloom. But the real relief was the earthy coolness here. There was furniture of the crudest sort, meager but substantial: a table and a bench made of rough narrow puncheons, and a pair of equally makeshift armchairs with rawhide weave seats. The table was set for two, he noticed, and in the middle stood a blackened pot full of a cold, grease-scummed stew, never touched. The big stone fireplace was flanked by shelves which held pantry goods and a few battered utensils. A single wooden cot stood in one roughly angled corner of the niche. From the careless litter of clothes and gear around it, this must be the father's bunk. He supposed that the other rear corner, where a curtain made of jutesacks sewed together had been stretched wall to wall, formed the girl's own compartment.

The exposed bunk was covered by a faded and ragged patchwork quilt which would be little the worse for blood-smears; he laid Jesse on it and straightened his legs, then looked around for water. He found it in a huge clay *olla* set deep in the cool shadow by the back wall. He drank deeply and greedily, and water had never tasted better. Filling a tin cup for

Jesse, he held it to his lips, letting some dribble on his chin, but provoked no response now. Jesse was pale and drawn under his whiskers; there was an inert looseness to his body, and a chill of real fear ribboned through Calem's belly. The bleeding might cease now that Jesse was unmoving, but he would need some competent help and soon.

Miss Charley came in; she moved to his side and studied Jesse, her pugnosed face grave and still now. 'He pretty bad, eh?'

'Bad enough. Now let's see where your pa is.'

She hesitated a bare moment, then shrugged. 'Why not? Want to let your horse cool off some before I set out. There's time.'

'Whereabouts is this mine?'

For answer she moved over to the curtain, nodding him to follow. She lifted the smudged cloth and ducked under it. Puzzled as he followed her, Calem found as he had guessed that this was her personal cubicle. There was a cot and a wall peg with some clothes hung on it, and a shelf containing toilet articles and a few gewgaws. A second jutesack drape, till now concealed by the first one, hung across the back wall. Before he had time to wonder at this, she stepped over and lifted the second hanging.

It covered a timber-cribbed opening, he saw, and beyond yawned a black tunnel that appeared to penetrate into the ridge. He understood then that this dwelling had been deliberately and laboriously planned to conceal the mine entrance and tunnel. A mine that had to boast a fine strike to justify this elaborate concealment of the diggings . . .

'Pa?' Miss Charley called into the darkness. 'You all right in there?'

'A course I ain't, dammit,' crackled a voice diffused by hollow echoes. 'Not pinned like a goddam—*hah!*' The voice exploded in a hollow, racking cough which ended in a wicked curse.

'He's all right,' she told Calem, then called: 'Pa, you light that lantern now so's we can get to you.'

After a moment a match was scratched alight, making a sulphurous flare far down the tunnel. It died to a low flame which a moment later grew on a lampwick in a wide pool of light that reached into the passage, picking out the straight rugged walls and timber cribbing. Gingerly, Calem followed the girl inside, ducking his head under the low beams. The air in the tunnel was as cool and clammy as a slug, and a stale-sweet odor of decaying wood clung to it. They picked their way into the fan of light, and she dropped to her knees beside the lantern.

The man was sprawled belly-up as the fallen timber had pinned him, half-twisted on his braced elbows and peering up irascibly. Some water and food had been left within his reach.

He was about fifty, a gaunt bantam of a man who would probably not top a hundred and twenty pounds sopping wet, but even flat and motionless there was something vibrant and restless about him, as if he were muscled with bunches of taut wires. He was, Calem guessed, as tough as cactus inside and out. His long bleached blond hair was like old hemp; his face was like an aging elf's, round and ruddy, but there was nothing elfin about his eyes. They were the color of wash-faded denim, and they looked old as sin, more shrewdly calculating than any eyes Calem had ever seen; he wondered if this were an illusion made by lampcast light and shadows.

'You hurting at all, Pa?'

'Goddlemighty, girl, what you think? Man my age takes the cold cramps in his bones has got every ailing since age five acting up. Can't feel a thing in the legs though, which is worrisome. You fool girl, you ain't brought but one man.'

Miss Charley said, 'Two,' and launched into an explanation which did nothing to sweeten Ethan Jacks' disposition. Meantime Calem dropped to one knee by the downed timber, laying a hand on it, feeling its heavy solidness impregnated by dampness. He wondered fleetingly where Jacks had obtained such timbers—not from that scrub growth in the valley below.

He saw that the supporting stull of this

87

massive overhead beam had given way, probably from a disturbance of the tunnel flank where Jacks was test-pitting. Most of the stull projected from the heap of rubble which had plunged from above, barely missing the miner. The overhead timber had not missed; it lay diagonally across the tunnel, half-blocking it; the upper end had slipped its stull, but had wedged against the tunnel wall, and so was prevented from dropping farther. The lower butt had plunged nearly to the floor, embedding itself in the loose earth and rubble which had tumbled over Jacks' legs. Had the butt caught them innocent of the insulating earth, or had the beam not gotten hung up on one end, the weight and impact would have crushed flesh and bone to a jelly. The timber was massive and solid of itself, and still supported a burden of rock that had been the roof. For a number of sizable boulders had fallen and a huge one had wedged itself between the wall and the beam's topside, an immovable weight. Apparently it had rendered the timber immovable too, as Calem verified by testing his strength on the timber, leaning with both hands.

'Was squatting under her,' Ethan Jacks said. 'Jumped when she give just in time, only not quite.'

Calem said, 'You move your legs?'

'Right one anyways. Left one's caught square under the point of weight. No break that I can tell. No pain without I pull hard. Not moving her without timber is moved first though.'

'You try digging away this loose stuff?'

'Told you before,' Miss Charley said with an acerbity that matched her sire's. 'Get the wax out, bub. I tried cleaning off the rock and like to brought the whole tunnel down on him.'

Calem braced a palm against the block-shaped key rock that wedged the timber down, sizing it, and she said disgustedly, 'You'll never budge it, bub, and you'll pull down all that rock behind it if you do.'

Ignoring her, Calem said, 'How about digging under your leg?'

'Tunnel floor is solid rock here.' Jacks watched him a dry, curious moment. 'You propose to flood the place and float her off, boy? You figure to witch up some water? Heh?'

Calem, his patience about played out from the acid needlings of this pair, said thinly, 'I'll wait till I get my growth.' He pointed to the space under the hung-up end of the timber. 'Look. Room enough for one man to get his back and shoulders under; that's the only way it will ever lift.'

Ethan Jacks rasped a palm over his stubbled jaw. 'Mebbe so. What you say, Charley?'

'One man ain't enough,' she said coldly. 'Time we quit jawing and I forked that horse. You keeping your word, bub? Damn, you better!'

'If it comes to that,' Calem said. 'But you better consider something else.' He looked directly at Ethan. 'Seems someone went to a sight of bother, building that room smack against this tunnel to hide it. If your girl fetches a posse from Mercyville, it will spill the beans. This here is a lonely place, only the two of you, easy pickings for any tough nut. How you know you can trust these Mercyville men?'

'How we know we can you?' Miss Charley countered flatly.

'I'm only one anyhow,' Calem said, his irritation deepening at her persistent antagonism.

'Good thought. Don't be so damn sudden, girl.' Jacks' shrewd eyes gleamed, eying Calem. 'Good shoulders on him. Mebbeso.'

'Worth a try,' Calem said, and nodded at the girl. 'She has got to lend a hand like I tell her.'

Miss Charley scowled; Ethan rubbed his beard again, saying, 'No feeling in the one leg. Pinched-off nerve. Another full day and night while you fetch help'd be too long, Charley. Like to lose a leg, of which I need both. As lief take the gamble and let Gault make his try.' He added with a snap, 'You do what he tells you, hear?'

She knit her brows, biting her lip; Calem met her angry stare with his face composed against a sick worry. Jesse needed the help of skilled hands, and if Jacks' were only half-skilled, he'd have a fighting chance. But he needed tending now, not tomorrow.

Miss Charley gave a slow, grudging nod. 'Reckon a lot of men would be no help. All right.'

Calem laid hold of the fat stull projecting from the rubble and worked it carefully free. He selected a cake-sized rock and set it near Ethan Jacks' thigh close to the big timber, and thrust the stull end between the down-angled beam and the rock. Using the latter as a fulcrum, he leaned tentative weight on the stull. Dust sifted from the roof. The stull made a lever that would add strongly to his own effort.

'You get on that,' he told the girl. 'Put your weight to it when I tell you.' He moved to the low gap under the upper timber, and flattening his bent back along it, said, 'Now,' and exerted slow force, lifting. He heard the gritty grind of rock on rock, and felt a faint, shifting lurch in the ponderous weight. 'Try to move,' he said.

He heard a grunting effort, and Ethan said, 'Dirt moved some. Legs don't.'

Calem's back was tight-braced and straining, and now he sucked breath into his lungs and sighed, 'Again,' and reached for a wellspring of power he wasn't sure he owned. His muscles shuddered with strain; the breath congested in his chest, and his head felt ready to burst. He heard the sudden rattle of falling rubble, and Miss Charley cried, 'Careful! You make it, Pa?'

After a moment Ethan grunted, 'No feeling in my goddam legs. Been buried too long. Lend a hand, girl.'

Calem told her, 'Go ahead,' and felt her let up slowly on the lever. Now the full weight of the timber was on his back, and he could only brace himself shudderingly while a surge of blood darkened his eyes and his muscles screamed for release from the bone-deep ache of exertion. And then he was aware that Miss Charley was back on the lever; the weight eased slowly. Not able to turn his head, he gulped, 'Is he out?'

She said yes, and now by agonizing inches they let the timber gently settle till the end struck solidly against the wall and was braced there. He dropped his shoulders, holding his breath; a little more earth and rock fell, and that was all. His legs went rubbery as he crawled from under the beam, and he simply sank to the ground, sweating and shaking and wondering how he had done it.

CHAPTER EIGHT

'You two give a hand,' Ethan said, 'and I can walk.'

With the girl on one side, Calem on the other, they hoisted him to his feet; Calem

92

carried the lamp in his free hand as they maneuvered down the tunnel.

He judged that Ethan had not dug the tunnel nor raised the massive shoring timbers by himself. Yet he and his daughter appeared to be alone. If others had been involved with these two, where were they now? It was not the sort of speculation that rested easy in a man's craw.

By the time they reached the tunnel exit and came into the big room, Ethan was able to move by himself, limping slightly. He hobbled around rubbing his thigh, and said with a grudging nod at Jesse, 'Say you want me to look to him?'

'Yes, sir. Your girl has said you know doctoring.'

Ethan gave a wheezing chuckle. 'Can tackle a case of colic or gallsores with a fair knowing hand, sure enough. He don't look like no horse or steer to this child.'

An animal sawbones. Calem favored Miss Charley with a tired glare. She was standing by the window, her rifle again in hand; she met his eyes with a cool and impudent malice. 'I fancy critters above a hellsmear of people I have met,' she observed. 'Pa, I give my word, so you look at him.'

'You got no business committing me,' Ethan said testily. His pale blue eyes were bitter-cold with suspicion as they shuttled from Calem to Jesse.

Like he was seeing us both dead if he had his way, Calem thought. *He must have him quite a strike here.*

'Pa!' she said sharply. 'You hear me now. You could have lost a leg easy as not, you said so yourself. Maybe even died, but for this here man. You owe him a proper favor.'

'Ain't said I didn't,' Ethan said surlily, staring bleakly at Calem. 'One thing. Want you both out of here by day after tomorrow.' Not troubling to disguise his reluctance, he moved to the cot.

The flesh of Jesse's leg, as Ethan bared it, was swollen and discolored, and the wound was a livid purple around the edge. 'Bullet went clean through, that's something. Best cauterize. Clean him up, Charley, whilst I heat the iron.'

Ethan got a blaze going in the fireplace, and while he was occupied, the girl set out clean rags and sweet oil and a basin of water. Her hands were quick and competent, even gentle, as she bathed the wound; Calem stood by, feeling ten thumbs' worth of useless awkwardness. There was really nothing for him to do, and he edged over to one of the windows; he was surprised to see that the sun had canted high to the south, and it must be close to midday.

This posed a sharp reminder of Dembrow, who by now might well have caught up with at least some of his stampeded horses. Calem's

94

jaws ached with a hard compression; as sure as sunset Dembrow would be closing the distance between them, and no telling how close he was by now. If not for Ethan Jacks' suspicion he might have left Jesse here and pushed on alone. A moment later it occurred to him that after what had happened with the horses, Dembrow might not be satisfied with only Calem Gault. He also began to worry that in his anxiety to get help for Jesse he might have brought danger and an unwelcome involvement to the Jackses. Yet, struggling with bitter uncertainty as to his next move, he said nothing.

The fire had died down; the banked coals glowed under a fine layer of ash. Ethan rummaged through a tray of cutlery and selected a steel carving knife; he thrust the blade into the cherry coals. When the wooden hilt began to smoke, he wrapped a rag around his fist and pulled it out; the dull-glowing blade steamed against the air as he carried it to the cot. 'Your brother's arms, Gault. You, Charley, take aholt on his ankles.'

Jesse was mumbling in quasi-awareness; his face had a dead pallor about the black slur of his beard. Calem drew his breath and leaned hard as Ethan lowered the blade. Jesse's body arched against their hands and his eyes flew open, varnished with fever. His breath sighed in and left him in a scream. Ethan said meagerly, 'Turn him over,' and after doing so and leaning again, Calem felt his guts wrench with the hiss and stench and trailing, muffled moan. And then with relief felt Jesse go limp under his hands.

'Sit down, bub,' Ethan said, 'before you fall down.'

Calem was glad to sit down. He went slack on one end of the bench and watched Jacks cleanse and bandage the seared thigh. He decided that, horse butcher or not, his daughter had not exaggerated the skill in Ethan's small sinewy hands.

Phlegmatically Ethan finished the dressing and, leaving Miss Charley to clean up the mess, went past Calem to a rickety washstand and filled a basin from the small water *olla* there. He said waspishly over his shoulder, 'you can stay over tonight, tomorrow. He better be fit to ride day after, because you're driftin' then.'

Calem stared at his big hands flat on the table, feeling in the wash of reaction a bitter worry flavored with guilt. He could not stay here and expose these people to the danger his presence meant, but could he desert Jesse? *The day after!* Jesse would not sit his saddle for a good week . . .

You got to tell them the truth, he thought, and swung restlessly to his feet; he rammed his hands in his hip pockets and began to pace. *They won't be happy with it, but they would find out when Dembrow comes anyhow. If I can get 'em to care for Jesse before I push on, that's better than nothing.*

Then, moving past one window port, he glanced out and froze, his heart almost stopping. The open port commanded a clean view of the slope below and the timbered valley, and beyond that the conical ridge he and Jesse and the girl had crossed to reach here. And now at once he picked out the riders jogging in a slow file around the curve of the ridge, coming off it down the long approach to the valley. For a cold long moment Calem did not believe it; he realized then that more time had elapsed than he had known, that Dembrow's driving fury to run him to earth would only be inflamed by knowing that one half of his quarry was disabled.

Miss Charley said, 'Pa,' in a breathing whisper, yanking Calem's glance around. She was standing by the other window staring out, and now she wheeled toward him.

'Them men. They the ones?'

'Yeah.' Calem felt the color rising into his face under her merciless gaze. 'I reckon I knew they was coming.'

'I reckon you did.' She turned abruptly to her rifle leaning against the wall and arced it around to bear on him as she swung back. 'I ought to shoot you,' she hissed. 'By granny, I ought to save them the job!'

Ethan Jacks came to the nearest port, muttering, 'What the old Billy Hell,' and

97

peered out. His slight form stiffened, and Calem felt his wicked glance then. But he did not take his own eyes off Miss Charley. Her rifle was level with his belly, and this time, her eyes blazing with a pale anger, she looked ready and willing to shoot; he was careful not to stir a muscle.

'Pa,' she was almost inarticulate with rage, 'them men is after him. He said he had shook them off and here they are not an hour hindmost! By granny—'

'Quit that cussin',' Ethan said curtly and, still looking at Calem, jerked his head toward the door. 'Get out.' Calem held stubbornly still, his feet apart, and Ethan yelled, 'You hear me? Light a shuck. Drag it. Slope. Hit the trail!'

Miss Charley said ominously, 'You better do it, bub,' shifting her rifle slightly.

Calem looked from one bleakly hostile face to the other, and said resignedly, 'All right, but my brother will need care. They're wanting me, not him.'

Ethan said, 'That's too goddam bad,' with what seemed close to a wicked relish.

'No, that's suitable,' the girl said abruptly. 'We owe him one life, no more.' Ethan growled under his breath, but she did not look at him. Her eyes were hard and unrelenting on Calem; she motioned with her rifle at the door.

Calem moved to the door and opened it; he

scanned the flinty slopes all around, gauging his best chance. To saddle and ready a tired horse and make his way off the slope before Dembrow was on him was out of the question. He would stand a slightly better chance afoot, retreating deeper into the brutal, barren country he had seen to the east. In that broken wilderness even Abel Sutter could not hold the track of a lone man bent on losing himself. There, horses could not follow the trail he would set; a man could somehow live off the land . . .

Obscurely he knew this was the desperate, driven mental state of a man with his back to the wall, but he did not hesitate. There was no time to think about it. He turned back into the room and picked up his saddlebags dumped beside the door, slinging them across his shoulder.

Then, as he straightened, Miss Charley flew in front of him; she slammed the door and shot the bolt, almost dropping her rifle. 'No. Don't you step out that door, bub.'

'You crazy, Charley?' her father shouted. 'He done his best to fob off trouble on us! You buying it?'

'No help for it.' Her young face was a shade pale, but she did not sound excited, only positive. 'I won't see no man thrown to a damn pack of wolves. Right's right and wrong's wrong, and that is wrong. I know that much, Pa, so don't say different. He's staying.'

'Hell he is!' Ethan swung violently toward the wall where an old Henry rifle lay across pegs, but her hard low, 'Pa!' brought him up short.

When Ethan turned, the rifle was centered squarely on him. His face worked like seamy dough. 'You raised your hand against your pa. You should of been learned a woman's place, by God.'

'Like you learned my ma?'

Ethan's faded eyes flinched; he muttered, 'No call for that. I have got your good in mind.'

'I ain't going to argue about it,' she said with an utter finality. 'I don't give a rap if these men pull a mountain down on us. We ain't sending him out there to be killed. You say more on it, and I'll hate you forever.'

Her manner was artless and simple and fierce, implying a startling and primitive innocence. It was as if she had never heard of filial respect or womanly meekness or moral compromise, and not knowing, simply spoke her mind and made her stand, and go hang to the consequences.

'Damn girl,' Ethan said in a haggard way, and turned back to the port, his stiff-humped back eloquent of the rage knotted in him.

Calem went to the pile of their gear and dug out Jesse's fieldglasses and, lifting his rifle from its saddle boot, returned to the window. With Miss Charley crowded beside him, he trained the glasses. By now the riders were pushing through the scant timber, and he could see the hunched, wizened form of Abel Sutter in the lead, bent low in his saddle to study the ground. As they left the timber close by the slope, Sutter straightened and looked up at the ridge; at once he reined back beside Major Dembrow and spoke, and the Major raised his arm for a halt. Sutter had spotted the 'dead house' and had guessed the truth at once.

Calem held his glasses on the Major, who was listening to the tracker now. Dembrow's whipcord breeches and linen shirt were discolored with filth; a white stubble rimmed his jaw, which was ridged and jutting with an inheld tension. His one bleak and frosty eye showed nothing. Calem moved the glasses along the men ranged behind him—Perc Tucker, Severo Cortez, and Wash Breed, all top hands and handy men with guns, all with a tough, unquestioning loyalty to their brand— and bringing up the rear, Frenchy Duval and Cody Dembrow.

Briefly, curiously, Calem let the glasses linger on the broad face of Dembrow's nephew. Everyone knew that Cody was kin from the wrong side of the blanket, but that told nothing. Always a cautious air clung to Cody's manner, and while he blended like a desert lizard into any situation, a man could sense more behind his sleepy, deep-lidded gaze than Cody let on. Now he had joined the consultation, and while the Major might well be arguing for a direct frontal charge up the bare slope, Cody was no doubt advocating a more circumspect action.

'Stand away,' Calem muttered to the girl, and settled his rifle barrel on the sill. He aimed and shot, and dust puffed from a rock a yard from the nearest rider. It made up their minds in a hurry, and they piled from their saddles and scrambled for the shelter of boulders.

Ethan said wickedly, 'Now what did that get you?'

'Time, maybe.' Calem scrubbed a palm over his sweating forehead. 'What you're thinking, I could of dropped him. About why he's after me, I'm in the right, if that makes any difference.'

'It don't.' Ethan spat through the port. 'Man who minds his own stays out of trouble.'

Calem clamped his jaw on further talk, staring downward. About a half-minute later Abel Sutter stepped out to sight; he held both hands over his head, his rifle in them, and a white silk handkerchief that was doubtless the Major's fluttered from the barrel.

'What's that for?' Miss Charley said with interest.

'He wants truce talk.' Ethan rubbed his knuckles along his whiskered jaw, thoughtfully. 'I wonder would he abide by that thing if a man went out?'

'He would,' Calem said unhesitatingly, thinking of the Dembrow honor.

Ethan gave him a swift, sly look. 'That so. Who you say was on the right side of the fence?'

'Well, he thinks he is.'

Ethan snorted, 'Don't we all,' and tramped to the door. 'Can maybe dicker 'em out of something.' He sounded almost tractable, and Calem felt an instant wariness.

As Ethan tramped down the slope, Abel Sutter catfooted upward to meet him. They met halfway, two undersized men, each beaten by his own harsh way of life to a rawhide mold. They talked for a long while, and Calem's grip began to ache around his rifle. But his feeling now was one of vast impatience; oddly he felt at last a strange calm freedom from overbearing tension. He had turned finally at bay, seasoned by the cold fatalism of a hunted man, ready to face whatever came.

The two broke off talk and split apart, and Ethan tramped hurriedly back. After entering, he barred the door by sliding a small timber into two brackets that were bent iron spikes anchored to either side of the entrance. Then he went to a shelf, took down a stone jug, shook it next to his ear and uncorked it and pulled deeply.

'Pa, what did he have to say?'

Ethan lowered the jug and eyed her with a

kind of benign hostility, then drank again and slammed the cork home with the heel of his palm. He seemed to be extending the moment with a secret pleasure. 'He says Major Dembrow says to send out these Gaults and we won't come to injury.'

'After you straightened him out on that,' Miss Charley said coldly, 'what then?'

'Says they will take 'em the hard way if need be.' Ethan drew his sleeve across his mouth, a sly malice filling his glance at Calem. 'What else he said, you killed the Dembrow boy in a way made it as good as murder.'

Ethan seemed to relax and expand with the liquor; he grinned slowly. 'What this Sutter said was this Dembrow's foreman seen it and claimed Dembrow's boy defended himself agin your pa. An even break.'

'I seen it myself. I say otherwise.'

'All right,' Ethan said cheerfully, as if the matter were of no account. 'Sutter says he tracked you all the way and he figures the hurt man with you is your brother; he allus had a swagger to his sign. Reckons it was him, this Jesse, that shot his horse, too. I asked him why he figures all this. Says because this brother of yours is a known outlaw and knows the tricks.'

Feeling Miss Charley's alert stare, Calem said lamely, 'He has skylarked some.'

'Skylarked!' Ethan shook his head with an explosive chortle. 'Well, that do beat all.'

'Anything else?' Calem said coldly.

'He says to tell the one shot his hoss that he don't need to worry about Major Dembrow hanging him. Says he means to call his own turn on that boy.'

Ethan moved toward the curtained alcove that hid the tunnel, and entered it. Calem sank onto the bench, rubbing his eyes. A tired disgust washed through him. He was sorry to embroil these two Jackses, at least the girl, but what else could he do? This fortlike place gave him a slender chance; out there he would stand bare-handed against six guns.

Another thing that troubled him was the hint of a sly satisfaction behind Ethan's manner after his talk with Sutter, and he thought with an increasing unease, *Suppose they made a deal of some kind?* All he could do was wait and watch.

Mingled with a deep distrust of Ethan Jacks was his worry for Jesse and a concern for when and how Major Dembrow's next move would come. Dembrow had come a long way, and now that his quarry was cornered, would he simply wait and starve them out? *I wouldn't*, Calem thought, and he knew with conviction that neither would Dembrow.

CHAPTER NINE

Through the long day Calem let the girl have the care of Jesse, who tossed and raved in a high fever. He was aware that he had little of his father's fine curative touch for ailing things; with experience and maturity his big awkward hands might develop the deftness they lacked, but for now, he knew, he could serve in best capacity by mounting guard at a port. That meant simply keeping an idle eye on the slope below against any move by Dembrow.

At least they were well-prepared for either a drawn-out siege or a sudden attack. Miss Charley had told him that a good store of food had been laid in, and plenty of water too. The dwelling itself was built snugly within a niche of the ridgeside, shielding them to the sides and rear; an attacker could come at them only from the front.

Calem was still convinced that the Major, already galled with impatience and further fretted by hours of waiting, would be edged toward a dramatic move before long, and he tried to think how it would come. With only five men to back his play Dembrow would not launch a suicidal charge across fifty yards of open slope to reach the dwelling. *Not by day, but what about tonight?* But tonight the moon would be full, and even with a heavy cloud cover, men rushing the slope would be highlighted all the way.

Calem put his face to the window and craned his neck to see the looming rimrock that curved out in a generous overhang, providing shelter from above. It seemed solid, and probably nothing but a charge of giant powder could bring it down.

Several times as the hours dragged on, he almost dozed. He had slept in fitful, nervous snatches since this long flight had begun, and now with his body inactive, the toll of grinding exhaustion was catching up. His eyes burned and throbbed from staring at the flinty glare of the slope.

His thoughts drifted; he jerked to full wakefulness at Miss Charley's quiet, 'Come eat now. I'll watch.' He saw that twilight shadows filled the room, broken by a dance of light from the fireplace where a stew was bubbling. Its savory odor filled the room, but though he hadn't put away a solid meal in days, Calem was not hungry. His head ached, and there was a strange buzzing in his ears.

He glanced down the boulder-laced incline, now blurred by the gray web of dusk. He could see a ruddy play of fire-light around the Dembrow camp, set well off from the base of the slope, but the blaze itself, along with the men and horses, was hidden by a great abutting shoulder of rock. The camp was a long rifle shot from here, but the Major and his men were too seasoned hands to take chances.

Calem surrendered the rifle to Miss Charley, and afterward got a bowl and ladled hot stew into it. He ate slowly and without appetite. Shortly Ethan Jacks emerged from the tunnel which he had not left in hours, filled a bowl for himself, and took a chair at the table opposite Calem. His face was almost bland in its sly calm, and again Calem had the sense of worried distrust. *Maybe he is putting it on to make you worry.* Yet the elaborate trouble that Ethan had gone to in camouflaging his mine indicated that he might go to desperate lengths to keep its secret from outsiders. While the Gaults remained here and Dembrow was camped on his doorstep, the secret was in danger.

Ethan did not say a word through the meal, and after noisily spooning up the last of his stew, again entered the tunnel. Calem could not finish his bowlful, and the room seemed to sway unsteadily when he started to rise. He sank back on the bench, rubbing his face, and then felt a hand on his shoulder.

'You go on,' Miss Charley said gently, 'and get all the sleep you want. I'll stand watch.'

He looked up at her, and her small face was full of a tender gravity, the underlip pouting in the way of a concerned mother's. Somehow this, with his awareness of clogging weariness, seeped through him like a sudden weakness. He felt like a long-frozen man starting to thaw; his eyes began to smart and he fumbled for the words and then, not trusting his voice, nodded dumbly.

He fetched his bedroll and spread his blankets out on the clay floor by the cot; he sat and tugged off his boots, watching Jesse. At last, he thought thankfully, Jesse was resting well. His profile, erased of its tight lines in sleep, seemed incredibly boyish even under a black smear of beard. Suddenly he remembered a time years ago when Jesse had stolen in late to the room they shared, and how, getting up still later in the night, Calem had lighted the lamp and seen this same sleeping face, fresh and untroubled and serene. Later yet he had learned that Jesse had come in late from skylarking with a town girl. Grinning at the memory, then sobering with the thought that on his account Jesse now lay hurt and helpless, Calem felt the surge of old affection. *I'll stay with him like Ma wanted, maybe even point him right. I swear I'll try.*

He stretched full length on his blankets. The fire had burned low; its dim glow curved along the girl's half-turned cheek as she sat quietly by the port, the rifle across her knees. A warm breeze from the aperture feathered along his body, and soon he slept, deeply and dreamlessly.

*　　*　　*

In one of the semi-wakeful periods that come to even a heavy sleeper, he felt distinctly the sharp tug at his belt. He stirred, groaned, and rolled on his side; he heard a boot grate along the floor only inches away, and it was this sound that brought him finally and fully awake.

Ethan Jacks was about six feet away, and backing off farther. Calem's six-gun which he had taken was slack in his left fist; another pistol in his right hand was trained watchfully. Seeing Calem's eyes open, he rasped softly, 'Don't you bat a winker. I have got both your guns, and your brother's. My girl's, too.'

He backed over to the window, and Calem saw that Miss Charley no longer guarded it. Their weapons were heaped on the floor by the wall, and Ethan laid Calem's pistol by the others.

'Reckon you made a deal with Sutter,' Calem began, and Ethan hissed: 'Shut your mouth!' He shot a swift glance at Miss Charley's curtained-off alcove. 'She is sound asleep. Told her I would stand guard. No reason she should even know till long after you've went.' He waggled his pistol gently, the light washing wickedly against his eyes. 'You wake her now and I'll blow a hole through you that you couldn't plug with a fist. You going to?'

'No.'

The lantern from the tunnel stood on the floor, its flame bright and steady, and now Ethan picked it up and carried it to the door. He had to set it down, while holding the pistol on Calem, to free a hand for lifting the bar that secured the door.

Outside the wind was sharp; a hard gust promptly caught the freed door and swung it against Ethan's arm as he stood half-turned, almost throwing him off balance. He instinctively dropped the bar to grab at the door, and the thick timber clattered on the packed floor.

There was a moment's silence as Ethan froze in place, and then came Miss Charley's sleepy, 'Pa?'

'It's all right,' Ethan declared harshly. 'Dropped my rifle. Get back to sleep.'

She did not reply; there were small stirring sounds and then the curtain was thrust quickly aside. She looked almost lost in a long heavy nightgown, much like an aroused, querulous child. As her glance passed to Calem and back to her father, understanding hardened her eyes to alertness.

She said between her teeth, 'I might have known. So you'd stand watch while I got some sleep, would you? You—'

'I had enough of your sass,' Ethan snarled with a harried exasperation. 'You get back in there.'

'Not much.' She moved deeper into the room, hugging her arms; she nodded angrily toward the two brothers. 'How much is a gold mine worth, Pa? One life? Two lives? Or maybe three—mine too?'

'Goddam it, now you hush that talk! You ain't going to be hurt; I am seeing to it now.' He arced the pistol in Calem's direction. 'With them two gone, our necks is safe. I ain't letting us get shot to pieces on their account. We don't owe 'em a thing. Time you stood by your pa for a change.'

She took a step toward him, her voice low and fierce. 'How much did you owe my ma? She never asked for nothing but a decent way to live. Speak of that, how much you reckon I owe you for being pa to me?'

'There ain't no sense to such goddam chatter.'

'See how much sense there is to this.' She straightened one arm, pointing at the guns on the floor. 'I am going to stop you, Pa. Else you will have to kill me as sure as you are killing these two.'

'All I got to do is lay this gun acrost your head,' Ethan snarled. 'And by God, I will.'

She gave him a strange, wondering regard. 'Why, you surely would. But happen that didn't stop me, you would shoot me to keep your gold safe. Ain't that so?'

The warm draft plied the dying fireplace coals to fresh life; the guttering flames highlighted the murky strain in Ethan's gaunt face. 'No. You are way wrong. You don't know, that's all.'

He bent and seized up the lantern, and moved it back and forth across the open doorway. It would be seen plainly from the camp below, and this, Calem knew, would be his signal, pre-arranged with Abel Sutter, for the Skull men to move in.

In the pressure of savage desperation, he was ready to discount all odds, even the handicap of his prone position, and make a lunge for Ethan. The bitter foretaste of defeat was in his mouth, for Ethan could gun him before he was on his feet. Yet his muscles gathered and tensed for the try.

But Miss Charley moved first, rushing on her father with the quickness of a young tigress. Catching his gun arm, she fought it down with all her weight.

Calem swarmed to his feet and took two half-diving steps. He caught Ethan solidly in the short ribs with the point of his shoulder and heard the wind gush from the smaller man's lungs as he went down. Calem and Miss Charley fell with him; after a moment of furious struggle, Calem rose with the gun in his fist. He heeled the door shut and settled the bar in place. The lantern dropped by Ethan had landed miraculously upright, unbroken. Calem picked it up and doused the flame, and moved quickly to the wash basin;

113

with it he drenched the live embers in the fireplace. As the last cherry glow expired and the room ebbed into total blackness except for moonlight shafting through the ports, he heard the girl move quickly to his side.

Calem bent groping along the floor till he found the rifles, and he passed one to her, saying, 'Get to the window.' There was a soft groan in the darkness, and he added, 'He hurt much?'

'No. You bumped his head on the floor is all.' Her voice was grim. 'He better stay out of our way.' Her bare feet whispered away across the floor, and Calem pressed his face to the port.

The strong relief of moonlight bathed out every detail of rock and brush on the uneven slope, and he saw no movement along its whole length. But the campfire had been extinguished, and Calem thought, *They are watching down there all right; they seen the signal, but they know the idea went wrong. Question is, will they come on now or not?*

His moving glance came to fixed attention now on a dark mass of brush near the base of the incline. Had it moved . . . or was he seeing things? Almost at once another clump of brush made a distinct stealthy movement along the ground for a good two feet, moving upslope. Behind it he picked out the prone form of a man, just as a third clump shifted forward.

Calem kept his gaze in aching focus, hardly

daring to blink. One by one he isolated the six men in their various positions on the lower hill. Three of them had gotten nearly halfway, this before he had spotted the first betraying movement; the realization brought a wash of clammy sweat to his body.

Dembrow could not have been certain beyond a doubt that Ethan's true intent was not to close a trap on himself and not the Gaults; tolled onto the open slope by Ethan's signal he and his men would be plain targets for the rifles above. Taking no chances, he had put an idea of his own in motion, and it had nearly taken them totally unaware. The human eye tended not to look for what it did not expect to see; men sprawled belly-flat to the angle of slope behind mobile brush shields could snake upward in silence with few and unobtrusive movements. Even these might easily have escaped detection in the fitful moonlight till it was too late. Had they gotten near the shack, a concerted rush might have taken the defenders almost before they could get off a shot.

Not knowing if Miss Charley had the danger pegged, he whispered a warning, but she cut him off: 'I seen them. Think I'll tickle 'em out of that.'

She fired, and one tangle of brush gave a violent lurch. A moment later a man leaped up, and her second shot merged with Calem's. The man tumbled back, and his body rolled slack and inert down along a pale slab of angled rock and came to a stop. Now a confusion of yells and shots made bedlam of the night. Major Dembrow's voice crackled out, calling a charge, and orange stabs of gunflame broke the dense ground shadows.

They were coming on the climbing run now as Dembrow threw caution to the wind in his effort to salvage the attack. Calem heard bullets pock the 'dobe walls; two seared air through the port inches from his head. The near slugs and the screaming ricochet of one filled him with a fear for the girl and Jesse.

One man was within twenty yards of them, running low and pumping shots, wildly emptying his magazine. Calem's slug caught him in mid-leap as he bounded over an obstructing rock, and he fell with an odd, turning grace. At the same time Miss Charley beaded another man who dropped to his knees holding his arm.

The charge was broken.

But it was Cody Dembrow's voice, not the Major's, that now hoarsely called on them to fall back. The Major did not countermand the order. Calem watched the wounded man move downslope after his companions, stumbling as if in exhaustion.

For a long time they stayed by the ports, passing only a few bare words. And finally, certain that the attack was past, Calem wearily located the lantern and thumbnailed a match

116

to flame, and lighted it. The racket had aroused Jesse to a loud delirium, and Calem went to check on him.

He was burning up with deep fever and sweating profusely; next would come the alternating fury of wracking chills. At least the fever was on him in full tide, which meant that it had to break before long, for better or worse.

Miss Charley had stayed by the window, but turning now, he saw her watching her father steadily, and her bluesteel eyes were implacable. Ethan sat at the table holding his head between his hands, his stare bent sullenly downward.

'Didn't want you getting shot,' he muttered. 'I could of settled it without shooting.'

'You was thinking of your damn gold,' she said without inflection. 'Offhand I can't think of when you thought of anything but. Now you hear what I'm thinking of. I'm leaving you, Pa. If we get out of this alive, I am leaving for anywhere I can, so it's away from you.'

Ethan Jacks' squinted gaze lifted slowly. His face was like a brown and desiccated mask with brittle eyes, and he said at last, 'All right. Do what you goddam please. I ain't going to stop you.'

Jesse moaned in his fever for water, and Calem's eyes sought the big water *olla* on the floor. He saw that it was broken in several large pieces, the puddling wetness broadening in a muddy stain across the hard dry clay. A down-angling ricochet must have found it— and all the water that remained to them was a few tepid quarts in the small *olla* on the washstand.

Calem felt the sure, instinctive fear of a man raised in a region of little water and knowing what the lack of water meant. All Dembrow had to do now, if he only knew it, was wait out a few days. By that time the punishing heat survived on a bare dole of moisture would leave them too weak to fight off even a daylight attack.

CHAPTER TEN

Cody Dembrow squatted on his heels by the fire and filled a tin cup from the blackened coffeepot. Drinking, he watched his uncle over the rim of his cup. The Major was pacing back and forth, his head bent, hands clasped at his back. *Like a damned little Napoleon*, Cody thought, but he wondered . . .

To the world, even to those nearest him, Jeffrey Dembrow had always presented a hard and passionless face. A true cattleman of his time, his given word to another white man was his bond. The way he had built his ranch and fortune, by moving onto Indian treaty lands and bribing politicians to have the boundaries refixed, only made him bolder, not more ruthless, than the rest. It did not account for the shell he wore around his emotions.

But there had been his wife: latter-day gossip said it had been a love match from the first between the young cavalry officer and the general's daughter, and a determination to build a great thing for his bride had decided Jeffrey Dembrow to resign his commission. He had begun afresh with family influence and his own driving will; he had seized and borrowed and bribed, and his blunt answer to renegades, rustlers and squatters was a rope or a bullet.

Two years after their marriage, a year or so before the orphaned Cody had come to Skull, the young wife had died in childbirth. And for Jeffrey Dembrow then, there was only the son she had given him and the ranch she hadn't lived to see grow and prosper. Partly these things had filled the bitter void, but also they had channeled his fierce energy into the single-minded ambition of making Skull ranch a power in the territory, one that would pass into Ames' hands and his sons' after him, a dynasty of Dembrows unbroken . . .

Perc Tucker stirred, and a grunt of pain left him; he was sitting upright against a rock, cradling his thickly splinted and bandaged arm against his belly. The arm was broken at the elbow, and Tucker grimaced with the agony that a slight movement cost him. Still he was lucky. Wash Breed and Severo Cortez had also been in last night's charge up the slope, and had not come down. From here you could see their bodies sprawled as they had fallen.

We could all have got smoked down if I hadn't give the order to back off, Cody thought. *How far will he carry this?* He knew the answer: Calem Gault's bullet had shattered a Dembrow dynasty, and that driving, insensate energy of the Major's would not let him rest until Gault was run to ground, no matter if many died for it.

Frenchy Duval leaned against the broad slab that sheltered their camp, his legs crossed, idly whittling at a mesquite branch. He whistled thinly through his teeth, occasionally peering about from under his brows without raising his head. Nothing fazed Duval; he took his orders and bided his time. His lean, relaxed grace was like that of a large indifferent cat inscrutable to the world.

'Major,' Tucker husked.

Jeffrey Dembrow came about on his heel and regarded the man a long moment as if he found difficulty concentrating on him. He said finally, 'Yes.'

'Wash and Severo died for the outfit, Major. You ain't going to just leave 'em lay out there.'

'Later,' the Major said in a soft tone that brooked no argument; as he spoke he resumed his slow pacing, a stocky man whose face was a haggard-eyed mask. The ravages of time and ambition had never noticeably marked him, but a few days of grief and driving fury had aged him incredibly, Cody thought.

The Major halted and lifted his head as Abel Sutter dropped to view around an abutment of sandstone. The shriveled wolfer paced noiselessly into camp, squatted by Cody, picked up the boiling coffeepot in a calloused hand that was impervious to heat, and poured himself a cupful. Sutter had come on the besieged hill from behind to reconnoiter the shelving rim above the 'dobe shack.

Jeffrey Dembrow said impatiently, 'Well? Can we get above them or not?'

Sutter pulled at his coffee before answering. 'You kin get on the rim all right, Major, but that fort of theirn is snugged into the cliff. Man dropped a plumb line offen the rimrock, she would fall a good ways out from the base, away from them shooting ports. Gives them too good a angle of fire.'

The Major's one dead eye burned on him. 'So that if a man came down on a rope from the rim, he would be shot off it before he could get near the wall?'

'Might work loose a chunk of that rim and bury 'em, but she is fixed pretty solid.'

'That was a barbarous observation, Sutter,' Jeffrey Dembrow said coldly. 'How well do you think they are provisioned?'

'They ain't no telling. Being so far from a settlement, I would hazard that little gent has laid in a good grubstake, though he might be stretching end of it, all we know.' Sutter pointed at the gushing spring nearby. 'Track shows they take up their water from there. A goodly climb, so they likely carry a good deal at a time. They could be fixed a long spell on both counts, but they ain't no telling.'

The Major came slowly around, hands clasped at his back, to face the fire; he said in a harsh and peremptory voice, 'Cody.'

'Sir?'

'I want you to ride back to Skull. If you start now, you should make it before sundown tomorrow; you can travel back by the cool of night and be here before noon next day. Bring Ed Grymes and the entire crew. And something else—' The Major seemed to weigh his thought, his eyes squinting nearly shut. 'Bring dynamite, Cody.'

'There's some in the tack barn, left over from that road-blasting job.'

'Bring it.'

The wind is up, Cody thought, *and he has the smell of blood in his nose*. He tossed away his coffee dregs, set down the cup and rose, walking to his saddle.

While he was cinching it on his sorrel, Frenchy Duval came over carrying two canteens, Cody's and his own. 'I have filled these. You will need them both, I think, eh?'

Cody nodded, and Duval fastened the canteens to the saddle, eying Cody across the horse's withers. 'The Major pushes ver' hard,'

122

he murmured. 'He pushes too hard maybe.'

Cody said noncommittally, 'Maybe,' and toed into stirrup and swung astride.

Duval cocked his head, shutting one eye thoughtfully. 'More men will die. It is plain. I wonder who will be the last.'

Cody felt irritation at the hint of enigma, of matters unsaid, that frequently lurked behind Duval's words. 'What's that meant to imply?'

'Why, the last shot may not be fired at the young Gault. Maybe at the Major, eh?'

Duval was merely needling him with some peculiar and personal notion of amusement, Cody supposed. He gave the gunman a bare nod and rode out from the camp, quartering south.

Leaving the ridges, he made good time on the flat barrens while the late dawn still held the heat bearably low. He traveled steadily all that day and well into the cool evening before making a night halt. He broke camp before true dawn, and holding his sorrel to a strong but not killing pace, reached Coyotero Basin by late afternoon.

The cook's triangle sent its tinny clamor through the velvet twilight as Cody rode into headquarters and dismounted, stiff- and drag-footed, at the corral. He walked the horse patiently up and down, unlimbering his own muscles. The bunkhouse windows were lighted, and the crew would be at supper. Cody was hungry, but almost at once his glance was

123

pulled to the lighted windows of the main house parlor, and he forgot hunger. In a few minutes he would see Trenna Dembrow, and how much he really wanted to surprised him.

★ Ed Grymes came from the bunkhouse at his rolling, thick-bodied gait; he gave Cody a surly nod, saying in an odd, slurred voice, 'Heard you ride in. Where's the others?'

Cody briefly explained his mission, his easy tone blandly masking his contemptuous dislike of the Skull foreman. Grymes had been with Skull from the start, filling his boots as the Major's right-hand man, but there was no real bottom to him. His loyalty to the Dembrows had been his life; and later, like any tired old dog wanting only to lie out his days in the sun, fearful of losing his place, he had curried favor with Ames, the son and heir, by covering up his many raw escapades from the Major. Yet Cody had to wryly admit, *Maybe we're not so different, Ed and me.*

Grymes' broad face was stamped with worry. 'You have got the kid pinned in this place? No way out?'

'Not as I know of,' Cody said dryly. 'Ed, you tell the crew I'll give them four hours to get shut-eye; then we are heading out.'

'Tonight?'

'Major's orders.'

Grymes gave a surly grunt, wheeling away; he almost stumbled, and Cody thought with conviction then, *Why he's drunk.* Usually

124

Grymes was a hard drinker off-duty, but only then, and he carried his liquor well. *Something is eating in him for sure. Now I wonder . . .*

Cody turned in the sorrel, watered and grained him, and afterward headed for the main house. It was an old rambling fieldstone-and-'dobe affair which had housed Spanish grandees. He paused on the veranda to bat the alkali from his clothes and run a bandanna over his boots, then went in. The *sala* was a low room filled with dark heavy furniture and shadowy corners not touched by the lamplight that played on the bright woolen tapestries adorning the walls.

Trenna Dembrow sat in an armchair reading; she looked up in surprise and rose with a small, uncertain gesture. Cody said mildly, 'I'm alone,' as he shut the door behind him. 'Could use something wet and ring-tailed.'

'Welcome back,' she smiled, moving toward the liquor sideboard. 'Where is the Major?' Even under the mourning black she wore, she moved with a feline, full-bodied grace, and the warm tones of her face belied the prim bun in which she had done her pale hair. *The grieving widow*, Cody thought ironically. He scrubbed a palm over his unshaven chin; he briefly explained, and said then, 'Reckon I had ought to clean up.'

In his room he lighted the lamp and poured water into a basin. He peeled off his shirt and undershirt, scrubbed himself with a sliver of lye soap that seemed to take off as much hide as dirt and sweatsalt, then scooped up water and laved its wet coolness over his head and shoulders. It cut his exhaustion, and he was toweling himself briskly when Trenna came to the doorway. 'I brought the drink here.' The undercurrent of her voice was like a sibilant purr.

Cody sprawled at ease on the bed, his boots crossed, sipping the drink. She had brought him a cigar too, one of the thin pale brown Havanas that Ames had favored, and she held the match. A pleasant euphoria stole over him; he wanted to draw out and savor this moment, drinking Dembrow whiskey and puffing one of Ames' cigars lighted for him by Ames' widow. But Trenna's manner disturbed him; she stood with her hand on a bedpost, slowly twisting her palm on it, and something alert and feline in her gaze made his spine prickle.

'What is it?'

'We needn't pretend with each other,' she said softly. 'We know how it is with us. But one thing, Cody. I will never make a demure or docile little woman for any man. I have to burn hard and bright or I will go out entirely. I warn you now—don't try to lock me up as Ames did.'

Cody considered, inhaling the fragrant smoke and letting it out; then he shook his head. 'No, I'd never do that. I'd trust you with a free rein. Till I found I had cause not to. Then I wouldn't lock you up, I'd break your pretty neck.'

'Why—I believe you would.' She leaned above him with a small fierce smile, and he put aside cigar and drink, and pulled her down to him. The perfumed softness and firmness of her yielded and clung; her hands at first gentle became tense and taloned. The stirrings of sound in her throat chipped dimly at the edge of his consciousness which all-resided now in the working hunger of her mouth. Finally she threw back her head, her eyes hot and heavy-lidded. Her smile was moist and tremulous. 'If you could do what you said to me—then you can do what else needs doing, now.'

He frowned, his fingers working on her soft arms. 'What?'

'You can kill a man.' She leaned into him whispering, 'Think of how it will be, only the two of us. Or rather . . . Skull ranch and us.'

Cody blinked. 'The Major?' His scowl deepened; he pushed her away and swung slowly to his feet. 'How long have you been thinking like that?'

'When I remembered that you are the Major's one surviving blood relative,' Trenna murmured. 'While I am Ames' widow—who could contest our joint claim?'

'Have you seen his will?'

'Who but Ames would be the heir? Ames is dead, and he hasn't made a new will.'

127

Cody watched her face steadily, her skin deeply colored with excitement, her eyes bright and feverish, and he thought wryly, *A man misses a hell of a lot in a woman till something brings it out.* And he said: 'Now how do I stack up alongside Skull ranch?'

'Don't be a fool.' Trenna's voice was an angry outlash; she wheeled away a few steps, then turned on him impatiently. 'I was thinking of us, and yes, Skull ranch—why not? Why else would I put up with Ames Dembrow, let alone marry him? Why have you bided your time here, hating them, swallowing your pride, if not hoping for a windfall? Don't deny that the idea has crossed your mind!'

'Maybe,' Cody said. 'Maybe it has, but a man can cover plenty of ground between thinking and doing.'

'Cautious Cody,' she gibed. 'Or would afraid be a better word?'

Cody gnawed his lip, his thoughts narrowing. Often and restlessly he had toyed with the same idea, but never while Ames was alive in more than an idle and formless way. *But now there is only the Major.* 'An old man,' he muttered. 'He won't live forever.'

'He's not quite sixty. We could grow old ourselves waiting for nature to take its course; meantime what would we have?' Her skirt rustled to her quick step; she pressed against his arm, her voice a brittle hiss. 'Do you think that he would consent to his bastard nephew

128

taking his precious son's place with his son's wife? He's already enshrined Ames in his mind, and he would disown us both. I'm not waiting, Cody, for you or for a windfall. There are always greener fields for a woman while she keeps her face and body—they do not last forever.'

'A man's neck,' he said dryly, 'can snap in just one second. They hang you for murder.'

'Only if you let them catch you. Cody, those Gault brothers don't intend to give up; they will fight until they're dead. There will be plenty of shooting before you take them, and in the confusion a stray bullet could find the Major as easily as not.'

He stared at her a long considering moment. 'That could be a stiff risk.'

'But worth the stakes.' Her words were soft and breathing. 'The men will think the Gaults got him—or say the bullet took him in the back of the head, who can say with certainty who fired it or that it was not an accident? When will you get another chance like that? Will you be scared, Cody? Will your hand shake?'

'I reckon everything has its price.'

'Everything. But the terms can be very lenient.' She breathed deeply, flushed with her victory. Her hands lifted, fumbling with her hair, and it fell in a whitegold mass to her shoulders.

He smiled faintly. 'I only have four hours

129

and I could use some sleep.'

'Could you?' Trenna glided to the commode, and softly pursed her lips over the lamp. 'Or are you being cautious again? We needn't be cautious now, Cody.' She blew gently, and her voice sank with the lampflame.

CHAPTER ELEVEN

The one or two hours of sleep that Calem had achieved before the attack came had not even blunted the edge of exhaustion. Though half-drugged for want of rest, he stayed on guard by a port till a cold murk of false dawn crawled across the world. Then he started, to find Miss Charley shaking him by the shoulder.

'You was sound asleep. I'm rested enough and I'll take over.'

Earlier Calem had insisted that she get her sleep; now he gave only a dumb nod and groped through the paling darkness to his blankets. He lost consciousness within five seconds of stretching out. But the strain of a long night's violence and vigil made his sleep a restless pattern of gray dozings and fitful dreams.

When he came awake, again with a start, his head ached and there was a sour taste in his mouth. A mote-flecked gauze of midday sunlight patterned the floor; he smelled food and his stomach turned over. He got blearily to his feet, feeling the discomfort of stale, slept-in clothes, and started for the washstand. Miss Charley was by the fireplace stirring a simmering pot of beans, and she said without looking around, 'Don't waste water, bub.'

Calem groaned, remembering. He moved to the nearest port and stared dismally out at the empty slope and the shouldering slab that shielded Dembrow's camp. 'You should of woke me.'

'No need,' she said brusquely. 'A look-see down there now and then'll do for daylight. Sit down. I'll pour you some Triple X, and grub'll be on directly.'

Calem had already noted that Jesse was sleeping peacefully, and checking on him now, found that his fever had broken. There was a fresh dressing on his thigh. Calem sat at the table and accepted the steaming coffee Miss Charley brought him. He nursed the scorching metal cup between his calloused palms and drank most of the scalding liquid. It was black and strong, and he felt better already.

'Thank you for changing the bandage. He looks a heap better.'

'He'll do.' She brought the bubbling pot to the table, holding it by a stick thrust under the bale handle. 'One of them rode out after dawn. Across the valley and over the ridge. I studied him with your glasses. Big man with light hair.'

Cody, Calem thought, and scowled into his cup. 'He'd be going to fetch help. Major'll want more men.'

She brought plates and forks and set the table, then sat opposite him before putting her hard turquoise eyes on him. 'How long, do you reckon?'

'Depends, but I'd guess they will push.' He ladled a generous helping of beans onto his plate. 'A few days anyway. Anything else happen?'

'Only they sent that little old Sutter man up with his white flag asking could they take down them two we got last night. I said all right and a couple of 'em toted down the bodies. That was all.' The faint pucker lines of a frown clouded her tan face. 'That surely sets rough in a body's craw. You and me, we shot that one together.'

'I shot somewhat before you,' he said quickly.

'Maybe you missed. I made the mark all right.' She lowered her eyes, turning her food slowly over with her fork. 'I'm still hungry. Ain't that something?'

The alcove curtain parted and Ethan Jacks entered the room from the mineshaft, and took his seat with a bloodshot look at Calem. He filled his plate and began to eat, and there was no more talk.

Calem turned his thoughts to the dilemma that still faced him, trying to weigh and assess every angle. Dembrow could not know that a chance bullet had wiped out most of their water supply, or he might be willing to wait the few days necessary to give thirst its way. With abundant water they might have withstood a siege of indefinite duration, rushing tactics and all. *They won't try that again, not after last night, leastways just so. But it won't matter in a few days when we are too weak to fight them off.*

He considered the possibility of slipping out by darkness, getting his horse, and making a running break. That would at least toll Dembrow away from the Jackses, who might otherwise share his fate. Dembrow would not purposely harm a girl, but she could easily be hurt or killed before the last fracas was done. This fact alone almost crowded Calem to decision.

Several other considerations dampened the idea. Dembrow would almost surely post a night guard against such a contingency, and the alarm would be sounded at once; again he would be running ahead of the hound-keen senses of Abel Sutter, this time with only minutes between himself and the enemy. Even so, he might have accepted the risk for the others' sake. But Dembrow's ultimatum, as Ethan had received it from Sutter, included Jesse as well as Calem. And Jesse was in no condition to make the break . . .

Calem had no doubt that Ethan had conveyed Dembrow's message accurately. The

133

Major was simply restating the old law of clan vendetta. Blood to be paid in blood, and not merely the individual but all his male kin must render payment, the bloodline destroyed. Calem's own forebears had lived by that code for generations; a whole branch of the Missouri Gaults had been wiped out to a man in such feuds, and the legacy of bloody recountings his father had given him made a raw mark on his memory.

No. Even the danger to two people who had no stake in his quarrel, a reluctant and cantankerous man and a fiercely idealistic girl, could not outweigh his duty to a brother. The blood-feeling was deep in his own bones, and he could not leave Jesse alone to certain death.

'Ma'am,' Jesse's weak drawl abruptly broke the silence, 'I would 'preciate a cup of that java.'

Turning his head, Calem saw with surprise that Jesse was fully awake. His color was good and his eyes were alight with dark impudence. Calem rose and went to the cot, his throat thickening as he took the hand his brother held out. 'Jess . . . you look fine.'

'Man most always does,' Jesse said gravely, 'when he is not used to being waited on by no angel and about to have the pleasure.'

Miss Charley had come over with a cup of coffee. 'I don't truck with a lot of fool taffy, mister,' she said flatly. 'It is known to melt on a hot day. Here.' She thrust the cup into Calem's hands and returned to the table.

Jesse blinked a couple of times and had nothing to say as Calem, grinning, lifted his head and tilted the cup to his lips. For Jesse, that had to be a seldom reaction from a girl.

While his brother drank the coffee in sips, Calem described the situation. Jesse was attentive during the telling and asked a few questions, and then he yawned. 'I 'vow, still weak as a half-drowned cat.'

'You get some more sleep. Plenty time for talk.'

Jesse nodded and sighed deeply; he shut his eyes, and soon his breathing grew deep and even. Calem stood by the cot for a while, looking down at the drawn and sleeping face. Once again the crushing hopelessness of his dilemma thrust home; it would be days before Jesse was in shape to move, and by then . . .

Ethan Jacks gave an irritable, hacking cough as he choked on a wrong-way mouthful. *You greedy old son of a bitch*, Calem thought in a sudden and unreasoning anger. *That girl must have had a fine ma, else her ma knew a better man than you.*

He felt a swift shame for the thought; besides, Ethan owed him nothing but trouble, considering what he had brought to Ethan's doorstep. But somehow it galled him to watch the miner noisily wolfing down his food in an obsessive sweat to get back to his damned tunnel.

The tunnel. The idea seemed to grenade full-blown into Calem's mind, and with an impact that left no room for doubt or hesitation. Instantly he crossed the room and ducked through the two curtains into the mineshaft. He found the lantern on a stull-anchored peg by the entrance, and lifting it down, wiped a match alight and let the yellow flare pick out his way as he moved deep into the shaft. Reaching its end, he made some rough calculations in his mind's eye. He had not seen the far side of the ridge where shack and tunnel were sunk, but the ridge was not a sizable formation. Gauging the tunnel's length now, he thought with a mounting excitement, *It can be done.*

Footsteps grated over the littered floor as Ethan came down the tunnel into the lantern light, blinking and glaring his querulous suspicion. 'What'n hell you up to?'

Calem said, 'How long you reckon it would take to run this shaft clean through the ridge?'

Ethan continued to blink. He scratched his whiskers and muttered, 'By God,' and stepped past Calem, digging his fingers into the hardpan wall. He hefted a gob of soil in his fingers as if weighing the possibility. 'By God,' he said again.

'How long?'

'Depends what-all we run into. If nothing worse'n hardpan, say six yards to the outside, a couple-three days. But there's plenty rock in this stuff.'

'We can work shifts,' Calem said quietly. 'Day and night till we're through. The Dembrow man that went after help should be over three days fetching it, there and back. By then my brother will be fit to ride. Our horses are in the canyon back of this ridge; allowing Jesse's hurt will mean slow riding, we got a good chance to make Mercyville if the Major don't size things right in a hurry.'

Ethan scowled. 'This tunnel ain't the safest place to roust about in, rotten timbers and falling rock. And we got no exter timbers to shore up as we dig.'

'I'll dig alone if I got to,' Calem said grimly. 'And you won't stop me, old man. I ain't happy about fetching my trouble to you people, but it's fetched. I'm getting me and Jesse out alive happen I can, and you would do well to think on helping us on our way soon as can be. Before Dembrow rushes the place with a small army. Awhile after we're gone you can call to him we have got away; he can look back of the ridge for the tracks. He won't wait to settle with you since we're the ones he wants.'

'He or some of his men are like to be back,' Ethan snarled. 'The way I have this place set up, they can guess about the gold. But I ain't got a choice outside kicking your ass down the hill first chance.'

'You tried that once,' Calem said coldly.

'You got no choice at all. You going to help me?'

Ethan spat at a rock. 'When that colt of mine takes a notion in her, there ain't no argufying. Otherwise I would 'low to get you one way or t'other. All right.'

*   *   *

The bulk of the labor fell on Calem's shoulders, and he could put in a four-hour stretch of swinging a pick or heaving rock and hardly know a twinge. But he soon found that prolonged stints of heavy work left Ethan Jacks retching with fits of deep, shuddering coughs. It was apparent that he was a desperately sick man.

Considering that, and the fact that he must by now have accumulated a large hoard of nuggets or dust from his strike, he could surely afford himself a better life for what time he still had. Evidently the unalloyed greed of getting, and that alone, held a pure domination of the man. As yet Calem had seen no sign of gold, but the whole shaft was heavily test-pitted and he supposed that Ethan had exhausted some considerable sweat and cunning in finding and caching his metal.

Foot by foot they extended the tunnel, the stubborn hard-pan yielding steadily to pick and shovel. It was a bitter and frustrating job that had to be tackled slowly: the dislodging of a key mass of earth or stone might cause them to be buried alive. They repeatedly ran into huge chunks of obstructing rock. They carefully, patiently dug around these and worked them free, and lifted or rolled them out of the way; Calem could hardly budge some of them.

Jesse appeared to be on the mend; he ate a little food, wanted as much water as could be rationed him, and got a great deal of sleep. At his request his cot was moved beneath one of the ports where, by being slightly propped up, he could maintain watch during his wakeful times. This, by sometimes relieving the need for Miss Charley's presence, enabled her to help with the digging.

By afternoon of the second day Calem was becoming aware of the biting strain of unremitting labor and snatched meals and too little rest. Ethan had just come back on the job after six good hours of sleep, and Miss Charley told Calem to quit for a while. 'You'll be bedded down sick as your brother if you don't get a long sleep.'

Calem shook his head; there was no time for more than snatches of sleep, but he returned with her to the shack for a hot meal. Jesse was asleep. Calem straddled a bench and tiredly leaned his head against his palm while she brought him coffee and beans and biscuits. Afterward she poured a cup of coffee for herself and sat opposite him, studying him with the merciless candor that at first had made him fidget. Now it seemed so natural to her that he barely noticed.

'For all you are homely as a rail fence in a mud storm,' she said presently, 'you got a hell of a pretty brother.' Calem almost choked. She frowned as if considering the import of her words, then shook her head. 'What I mean, you have got a plain kind of face.' She promptly shook her head again, saying honestly, 'Nope. It's homely. It is nice homely, what I mean to say. Sure like to watch it. Can't fancy your brother's face even if he is fine-lookin'. Just something about the two of you. So almighty different, even though a body can't miss you're brothers. It's sure funny.'

Calem ate in silence for a full minute, and then said, 'You come here with your pa after your ma died?'

'Shucks no, boy.' She chuckled, an odd throaty little chuckle that it somehow tickled him to hear. 'I hardly 'member my ma; she died a long time back. Old pa, he was allus a restless scamp, I 'member that right enough.' The stormy little frown lines touched her brow. ' 'Mandy allus said that he drove her to her grave. Seems likely when I think on a lot of things. 'Mandy said that Ma just wore out following Pa's will-o'-the-wisps across the West. Reckon she meant the mother lode. He was allus tracking down one story after t'other trying to locate the mother lode.'

'Who is this 'Mandy?'

She said that Japh and 'Mandy Starrett had been an elderly couple who were the last citizens of a deserted mining camp where bonanza had come and gone. Ethan Jacks had left his ailing wife and small daughter with them. Shortly afterward Addie Jacks had died, and little Charlotte Lee had been raised in a remote, burned-out glory hole by an old couple too slowed and mellowed to discipline her. Of Ethan she had seen practically nothing over the years; he would drop in from nowhere without warning, buy a few supplies at the Starretts' trading post, and be off again on the heels of a fresh rumor.

About a year ago Ethan's wanderings had brought him to the isolated camp of an aged Mexican whom he found dying of cholera. He had cared for the man, easing his last moments. In gratitude, before he died, the Mexican had directed him to an aging, yellowed map hidden in his belongings which, the old man said, told the location of a lost mine in the territory, probably the northernmost of the old Spanish gold workings. At one time, when the Comanches began raiding heavily in the district, the Spaniards had their Indian laborers camouflage the mine entrance by building the facing wall of a prehistoric cliff tomb across it. Then they had cleared out with their jackloads of dust and nuggets. The Spaniards had never returned to their concealed mine; war came

141

and in its wake the territorial cession to the United States.

One of those Spaniards had been his *patrón*, the old Mexican insisted; he had died a broken man in Old Mexico, tired and discouraged, certain that the *Yanquis* would only rob him of his mine if he came back to reopen it. He had left the map to his faithful servant who had come here and scoured the ridges for many months, but had not yet found the hidden mine when he had fallen ill. Then, Ethan Jacks had suggested, wasn't the map false? No, but a man needed younger legs to clamber among these ridges; he needed undimmed eyes to locate an almost invisible façade in a ridge which was only an imprecise cross on a map.

After burying the dead man, Ethan had found the mine in a few days. Then he had visited Starrett's post to buy supplies. It had been a long while since his last visit; Japh Starrett had died and 'Mandy had allowed she would return to her old home in the East and take Charlotte Lee with her and raise her to be a lady.

'I wasn't going to be no lady, I can tell you,' Miss Charley said with satisfaction. 'Oh, I was grateful to 'Mandy and all, but I said I would go where my pa went after this. Pa, he groused some about that, but after all's said, I reckon he was feeling a touch lonely.'

Calem scraped up his plate. 'Seems I heard you offer to leave him last night.'

Miss Charley raised her tawny brows. 'You're damned well told I mean to leave him. Old Japh and 'Mandy, they learned me what's right and what's wrong. Pa and me don't see things the same at all, and I have figured what 'Mandy meant, how he killed my ma by not giving a damn. I can make my own way in some city.'

'Well,' Calem said, and paused to finish his coffee. 'You know, it is bound to be a sight different for you in cities.'

'I reckon so. You ever been in one?'

Calem thought a moment. 'St. Louis. We passed through St. Louis going West. I was a tad, and I remember the street lamps most. *Electric* street lamps, they was.'

'Sure enough? What's those?'

Trying to explain, he appreciated his own mind as a storehouse of civilized knowledge, despite his blank areas, next to hers. It was her lack of everyday facts that he took for granted which surprised him most, things like *McGuffey's Eclectic First Reader* and grace before meals and who was the first U. S. president. Her interest was lively and unflagging, and he needed to mention no fact twice. Still her innocence of social cautions was enough to land her in a peck of trouble in civilized places and keep her there.

Calem smothered a yawn as he stood up; he said abruptly, 'You know your pa has got wasting consumption?'

'No. What's that?'

'All that coughing, you didn't make nothing of it?'

She shrugged. 'He allus coughs. What's wrong with that?'

'Well, there was an uncle I remember back in Missouri coughed that way. He had a consumption which he died of.'

She was silent a long moment, her eyes lifting with a fierce grave honesty then. 'Reckon I got to think about this.'

He was starting for the tunnel when she said, 'You best sleep a few hours.'

He shook his head, saying, 'Can't allow the time,' and half-turned as he spoke. His eyes passed casually across Jesse's face and snapped back with a fine sense of shock as Jesse swiftly shut his eyes. An instant earlier they had been wide open, even though he was motionless, his breathing deep and regular as if in sleep.

It had been no moment of drowsy half-waking, Calem knew; there had been a total, animal alertness in that look, and he thought, *He tried to cover that he was listening. But why?*

If it were Miss Charley's talk of the rich-bearing mine that had taken Jesse's attention, the answer to why he was feigning sleep was as unwelcome as it was obvious. The thought came to him with an intensity of conviction of which he was not proud, but which he could not shake away either.

144

CHAPTER TWELVE

When he returned to the tunnel he found Ethan in a blue temper, staring at the fresh excavation and cursing in a bitter, savage, monotonous tone.

'What is it?'

For an answer Ethan raised his pick and hammered it into the tunnel end. There was a solid clank of metal on rock, and the pick fell away without scoring. 'We run smack into a dead wall, that's what.'

The great rock slab was nearly level across its face, extending wall to wall and floor to ceiling, as they found by knocking the loose earth from its surface. It was a bitter blow to their hopes, perhaps a total block to more progress. Since the boulder was too large to move, they could only attempt to find the shortest way past it, over or under or around, and hope that the impediment did not prove fatally time-consuming.

Calem found, by striking off great chunks of earth to either side, that the block curved inward on the right side. He began doggedly to dig, burrowing out a low narrow corridor along the flank of the slab. To proceed farther he had to wedge his body into the passage and, with no leverage to spare, hack awkwardly with his pick at the gravel-laced hardpan. As it fell away, Ethan, squatting directly behind him, scooped up the dislodged earth in a pan and fed it backward into the tunnel.

This was slow and grueling labor, and a clogging weariness dragged at Calem's muscles. Each exertion began to cost him a conscious effort, and he wondered if the slab would ever end. A bitter discouragement deeper than any he had known yet settled in his belly. How long had they been at it already, and how much of their precious margin of time remained before Cody Dembrow returned? He felt on the verge of collapse, yet he dared not quit for even an hour. *One more hitch as mean as this block-up, and we're done for sure.*

'You goddam fool,' Ethan burst out. 'Watch what you're doing!' He almost upset Calem, diving his hands between Calem's boots to paw wildly at the fallen earth. He brought up a piece the size of a marble taw and rubbed it on his sleeve. He raised it in a trembling hand, the light catching its dull sheen. 'See what you almost made me lose, goddam you? That's *gold!*'

Calem blinked and drew a gritty sleeve over his sweating forehead. He saw his hand was trembling, and suddenly all the exhaustion and harried temper in him let go, snapped his patience like a tenuous, drawn-out thread.

'My life,' he said thickly, 'is a sight more important to me than your damned greed. Don't you whine to me, old man.'

Ethan scrambled to his feet. He pulled a flat canvas pouch from his pocket and dropped the nugget inside, restoring the pouch to his pocket. Then he picked up a shovel and fisted it in both hands, snarling, 'You dirty pup, I'm of a mind to wallop some manners into you.'

Calem promptly emerged from the passage, gripping the pick, feeling the feral urge to smash at something. 'Come on, old man. Show me some manners!'

Ethan backed off slowly, his wiry body sunk into an agile semi-crouch. 'You touch a hair o' me and I'll split you wide open!'

'You go ahead and do it anyhow!'

'By God, I will!'

'Well, what you waiting for?'

'By God—!'

Over their shouting came a quick rush of feet, and then Miss Charley, flushed and furious, pushed between them. 'You stop that right now! I never seen such a set-to over nothing.' She wheeled on Calem. 'You ought to be 'shamed of yourself, a big fellow like you picking on a little old man.' Snatching the pick from his hands then, she gave him an angry shove toward the tunnel exit. 'You ain't in no fit way to work. Get up there and cool off. And get some sleep, you hear?'

'Little old man?' bristled Ethan, and his voice brought a little sand and pebbles sifting down.

She swung on him, her eyes metallic. 'Don't

147

you dast lift your voice at me ever. I won't have it.'

Ethan was sputtering like a chain of Chinese 'crackers, as Calem wearily passed out of earshot, trudging up the tunnel. But as he neared the exit he became, quite suddenly, alert and listening. The sounds as of someone rummaging about in the room ceased then, and an instant later he heard the cot creak. *That was Jess*, he thought in amazement. *He is up and about.* And then he knew the real answer: *The gold for sure. He was hunting for old Jacks' cache.*

Calem felt a sickness heighten the mild dizziness of his exhaustion as he stepped into the room. Jesse was sitting up and looking idly out the port; he gave his ready smile. 'Hi, kid. How's it go?'

'Poco-poco.' Calem stepped to the other port; he looked out at the rocky slopes and ridges where the afternoon heat hung like a shimmering veil. 'Jesse, I hope you can sit a horse in a day or so.'

'Hope so,' Jesse said laconically. 'Fetch me a drink, will you, and a smoke?'

It was a bitter confirmation. *Sure I will, just as if you couldn't get about.* He brought a cup of water, and Jesse's makings. Then he sat on the bench, set his elbows on his knees and laced his fingers together, grimly determined that the time had come to square them away. 'Jess, I want to talk.'

148

Jesse drank sparingly of the water, then began to fashion a cigarette. 'Talk away.'

'I been thinking about after we got out of this. I mean way after, when we have shook Dembrow off and can worry about something else.'

Jesse nodded absently. 'Like what?'

'Well, like where can we go from there. I had thought you might have an idea or two.'

'Hell.' Jesse expertly shaped and sealed the smoke. 'You go find Ma, and I'll go back to . . .' He gestured vaguely with a match as he thumbnailed it into flame and touched it to his cigarette.

'I guess there's no need to say it,' Calem agreed dismally. 'I was hoping you would want to stick by.'

Jesse waved out the match, squinting at him with a wondering irony. 'Why, I thought it was clear. Don't go trying to make me over, Cal.'

'Jess—damn you! Don't you ever think ahead?'

'A man always does, and I read the trail sign a long ways back.' Jesse's eyes pinched half-shut against the smoke. 'Some place there's a knife or bullet with my name on it. A man follows his nature, and it ain't a question of knowing. I may be stoking fodder for old Satan, but I mean to burn my own way till then.'

Calem said flatly, 'Time comes even a fiddlefoot has got to take root.'

'So much for yours,' Jesse said irritably. 'Now leave me to mine, will you?'

'Hell,' Calem said, his frayed temper snapping again. 'You never done anything a lick of good, not even yourself. Ma, I never seen her take a thing but grief on your account. I'll grant you stuck by me a while—'

'You don't need to,' Jesse cut in. 'You pulled me through the desert, that squares it, by God, so don't think you'll tell me my business!'

'I won't again,' Calem said tautly, and came to his feet. 'So long as your business don't touch these people. It's on my account you're here, and anything bad coming of it is on my head too. I know why you was rousting about before I come in; I ain't forgetting it, so you better not.'

Jesse's gaze darkened; he said very softly, 'I won't, boy, you can bet on it,' and snapped his cigarette to the floor in a shower of sparks. He rolled on his side, presenting his back.

Calem tramped to his bedroll and stretched out, throwing an arm over his eyes. He should not, when he was desperately in need of rest, have undertaken a crucial talk with Jesse. Yet, though he told himself that the damage done by the hot exchange could be undone in a cooler moment, he had the sinking sense that they had crossed a shadowy line of no return. That the talk had marked the end of something . . .

Sleep came imperceptibly, even as he was

thinking that he would not sleep now. A sleep that was deep and dreamless, with all sense of time and urgency blunted. He came drowsily and pleasantly awake, and was fully alert before he remembered and sat up with a start.

It was morning, and the smells of frying bacon and fresh coffee grabbed at his belly. He was not only fully rested but more ravenous than he had felt in days. Ethan, glowering at his food as he ate, did not look up as Calem sat down and Miss Charley brought his plate of food.

'You should of woke me long ago,' he said gruffly. 'This ain't no time to catch up on sleep.'

'You wasn't in no shape for much else,' she said tartly. 'Pa and me got plenty done meantime.'

He only nodded and bent to his plate; otherwise in argument he would have to look at her, and because he suddenly wanted to, he somehow could not. For the first time she had put on a right sort of dress made of a blue-and-white-checked calico. The skirt only hinted demurely at the flaring hips, but the bodice stressed the swelling breasts, confining the straining contours of them in a way which indicated that the dress, though bright and new, had been sewn for a younger girl. The tangle of her short hair had been combed out to a smooth palegold and tucked back of her ears by a blue ribbon. With the sharp contrast of her golden-brown skin and eyes of gunsteel blue, she hit a man's eyes about twice as hard as a girl who was merely pretty, which she still was not.

He caught Ethan shuttling looks between Miss Charley and him, causing him to brace himself for another waspish display. But strangely, Ethan looked more thoughtful than outraged.

When he and Ethan went together into the tunnel, Calem found that substantial progress had been made in his absence. A deep passage now curved entirely around the blocking slab and continued a full yard behind it. For a while they worked steadily, Calem whacking at the hardpan with careful strokes of the pick while Ethan scraped out the loosened earth, both freezing to immobility whenever a clod of earth or a trickle of pebbles fell from the sides or from above, which was often. At any moment a whole section of the unshored wall might collapse without warning.

'Enough for now,' Ethan said before long. 'Come on out.'

'No time.'

'No time, hell!' There ain't over a yard to go by my calc'lations. We don't want to bust out by daylight, and she won't be dark for hours. Come out of there. Got things to say.'

The two of them worked back to the original tunnel area where there was plenty of good safe shoring and room to stretch. Ethan

152

sank down on his spare haunches and produced a stubby pipe, motioning Calem to a rock. He sat down, leaning on the pick.

When he had his pipe going, Ethan said truculently, 'I decided. Ain't safe for Miss Charley and me here even after you're gone. Them yahoos you led here know of the place and have figured by now that something like gold is the reason for it.'

Calem stared at the ground in the pool of lantern light. 'Reckon it's time I said I'm sorry, though you won't give a damn about that.'

'Don't be so goddam sure of yourself,' Ethan said testily, and Calem looked up in surprise. 'Time you got something straight in your head. Ain't but one thing under the sun means a whoop to me, and that's her. My girl.' At Calem's openly skeptical look, he nodded grimly. 'The other night when they come up the hill and you handed her a rifle, she could of got killed. You think of that?'

Calem lowered his eyes. 'I did afterward.'

'I thought about it then, and plenty since. It had been in the back of my mind, but it hadn't stuck so hard till then, knowing she could be hurt or killed.' Ethan's pipe had gone dead, but he made no move to relight it. 'I follered the rainbow for most of my life, and now I found the pot of gold, it don't mean a damn thing but one. It can do for Charley, give her a grand living, good schooling too if she wants it.'

'Grand living?' Calem was skeptical still. 'You had a chance to give her just a good life, her ma too, plenty of chance. It's like she said, you never cared for nothing but yourself. Ain't that so?'

'It's so. Had my reasons for changing. I'm dying, Gault.' Ethan mechanically tucked away his pipe. 'Last year over on the Yellow I got shot by a claim jumper. Bullet is still in me. Went through my lungs and is so near my heart the sawbones wouldn't go after it. Told me a blow, something sudden like that, could kill me. Then I got consumptive. Only a question of time, and I want enough gold to see her fairly off.' He shook his head. 'That's all of it, Gault. Gold don't shine for a dying man. But I have put away enough now that we can afford to pull out. We'll go with you.'

Calem was puzzled. 'Seems you might better wait till we are gone and Dembrow after us. You got every reason to want to get shed of us.'

'You know the word of God, Gault?'

Surprised by the oblique question, Calem said slowly, 'The Good Book? Hope so.'

Ethan frowned, leaning forward and crossing his arms on his knees. 'My girl is shy as a colt on knowing the world. She is wild, sure enough, but like a fawn is. It is like she never ate of that fruit the Book tells of, and if somebody she fancied told her something it would be gospel to her.' Ethan shifted on his

154

haunches. 'I can make her well off, but I won't be around long. Sooner or later there will be a man. Wrong man could get her into a peck of trouble and nobody to stop it. Nobody but the right man, that is. Reckon you see now.'

'No.'

Irritably Ethan spat over his shoulder. 'Goddam it, I am saying you're the man, Gault. I been watching you. Handle yourself choicely well, and it is plain you still believe in God and goodness. There ain't never too many like you, so I am speaking out plain. I want your promise. Watch out for her, Gault. Take care of her.'

Calem said, hedging, 'She wouldn't hardly like that, you know.'

'Not off anybody, no,' Ethan snapped. 'That dress, though. 'Mandy Starrett made her that one nice dress a spell ago and she never wore it. She wore it for you, boy, to set herself off. You're 'most of an age with her; like calls to like, and that's as it should be. If there was ever a strong thing between you, I know you would do right by her. All I want to know now, do you like her well enough to see after her?'

'Yes sir, I—I guess I do. But I got nothing to give her.'

'Gold will take care of that. You take care of her.'

Calem shook his head in bleak negation. 'No. It ain't no good. There's Major Dembrow, and there will be hell to pay when

155

he catches up. I can't promise anything, knowing that.'

'Suppose you never had to meet him? Suppose you knew that?'

'I don't hardly see no way around it.'

Ethan thumbed back his wreck of a hat. 'I got a way maybe. Nor'east of here about a half-day ride there is a good piece of wild mountain country that ain't been touched except by Injuns, mountain men, surveyors and a few drifting men like me. A good ten years ago I was back in there and came on a great wide canyon with cliffs all around. Ain't but one trail to the bottom. There is plenty woods and grass in there, and good water. Plenty game, even stream fish. Struck me that with a few needs like shells and salt, a man could live in such a place for years and never be found out.' He paused. 'But you wouldn't need to stay there past two-three months till things quieted down. Then you could pull stakes for anywhere you had a mind to.'

Calem said nothing for a full thirty seconds, turning the idea over carefully. Ethan's proposition dovetailed with an increasing reluctance he had felt about going on to Mercyville, and there, with punitive law at his back, waiting for Dembrow and the showdown. He had already felt the gray distaste of embroiling the Jackses in his trouble; involving still others was bound to result in killing. Or he might forestall the final clash by running, always running, one step ahead of a man whose tenacious passion would let him bide his time for months, perhaps for years, while he hired detectives to track down Calem Gault wherever he went, under whatever name. Ethan had offered a way to cut off the relentless pursuit, swiftly and surely, and postpone a showdown for good.

But he said: 'That Abel Sutter, he can track an ant to its hole.'

Ethan's denim-colored eyes glinted. 'Can he track a bird? I can lead him over stretches he can't pick sign on because there won't be none.'

'It sounds good, sir. Thank you.'

'Got no thanks coming. I'm seeing to your neck on my girl's account.'

'Mr. Jacks, I am curious on one thing. You have talked like you expect to be leaving her shortly.'

'Man in my shape could any time, told you that.' Ethan had started to rise, but now he sank back on his haunches. 'Hell. You're right. I will see you to the canyon, then push on. Last my girl will see of me. Best that way.'

'Sir, that is a mistake,' Calem said bluntly. 'So is not telling her about your condition.'

'How you know that?'

'She wouldn't of said she was leaving you if she knew. She ain't that kind. She is the kind would want to know. She wouldn't thank you for keeping it from her.'

Ethan grimaced as if he had bitten into something sour. 'You heard what she thinks of her pa. Whatever she wants, I ain't got it to give. Too late to find out.'

'What she wants,' Calem said slowly, 'is to know her pa is got a feeling for her. What you got to give is time, the time you got left. Was I you, I would spend it with her. Let her know you ain't the man you was. She would want to know that too, more than anything.'

Ethan looked shaken; he said, 'Damn you, Gault. No more o' that.' He stood briskly, hefting his shovel. 'We will bust the tunnel through when dark comes. I can get us out of here then without being caught out. You got two horses. We will put your brother on one and take turns riding the other.'

Calem had been worried about the horses. 'Surely hope Dembrow ain't found them.'

'No fear of that. The canyon back of the ridge where they are is hid good, plenty water and grass. They will be rested and feeling sassy.' Again Ethan's gaze was hard and shrewd as he fastened it on Calem. 'I will turn the gold over to you before we split company. But mark you this: that brother of yours wants the gold. Has been scrounging about looking for it every chance. Got a feeling he would kill me for it. Might even kill you for it, Gault.'

'No,' Calem said coldly. But after a moment as the words sank in, he added almost angrily, 'Anyway I'll be watching him.'

158

CHAPTER THIRTEEN

Cody Dembrow, heading up the bulk of the Skull crew, rode into his uncle's camp at sunset. They were a tired and temper-edged lot as they offsaddled by the seep and walked their horses up and down before watering them. The ranch cook had accompanied them leading a pack animal laden with supplies, and he promptly set to unloading his utensils. Cody assigned a couple of men to remove a bulky case from the back of another pack horse, then tramped over to where Major Dembrow stood.

The Major was bareheaded; a warm twilight wind toiled with his white hair, and there was something tense and implacable in his stance. He said in a clipped and dispassionate way, 'The dynamite, Cody.'

Cody motioned toward the pack horse the two men were unloading, then fell in behind the Major as he walked over. 'Careful with that,' Cody told the men sharply. 'You ain't handling Roman candles.'

They gingerly set the case down, and the Major bent over, peering at the stenciled letters across the top: *Danger—High Explosives. This side up. No. 1 Dynamite— $1\frac{1}{4} \times 8$ in. 50 lb.* 'I got some blasting caps and fuses in my gear,' Cody said.

'I know nothing about setting off dynamite,'

the Major said curtly. 'But I have a use for it now. You've handled the stuff.'

'Sure.' Cody paused, glancing up at the loaf-shaped ridge where the cliff dwelling nestled under a heavy overhang. 'You want to pull that rim down?'

'As I've said before, no,' the Major snapped. 'I don't want to bury them; I want to take them alive if possible. I want you to blow in the front of that stone shack.'

'I won't need fifty pounds of dynamite to knock down a little mortared wall,' Cody said dryly.

The Major's hand made a chopping gesture of impatience. 'How much?'

Cody paused, considering. 'Can't get near enough to set a proper charge so the explosion is contained. Still, if a man got above them on that ridge, fused a charge and dropped it by the wall—I reckon one cartridge might breach it and not hurt anybody inside much. That's maybe, Major. A proper set one would blow them to kingdom come, that's for sure.'

'The chance they take by refusing to surrender,' Jeffrey Dembrow said. 'However, before you drop the charge, I'll call out my intention and give them a final opportunity.'

Abel Sutter had sidled noiselessly up beside them. He tipped back his hat, snuffling the air like a hound; he said, 'Be rain before long. Aplenty of it.'

'Tonight?' the Major demanded.

160

'About midnight.'

Jeffrey Dembrow rubbed his chin. 'A heavy overcast of clouds should be of considerable help. We'll wait till then.'

Cody unsaddled his mount and carried his gear off to one side. He spread out his soogans, tugged off his boots and, stretching out, folded his hands back of his head and let all his muscles go slack. He watched the last tinge of twilight give way to full night that dyed the sky to deep indigo and gave a solid shape of blackness to the land. The men had built up a half-dozen small fires and sat in slack clusters around them.

Over by the cook's fire the Major sat tailor fashion with his foreman, Ed Grymes, and now Cody caught the abrupt, harsh lift of his uncle's voice: 'Damn it, Ed, what do you mean by it's not too late to turn back?'

Grymes stirred uneasily on his haunches. 'Nothing, Major. 'Cep'n I would purely hate to see you get in trouble on this account. With the law, sir, and that's all I meant to say.'

The Major's answer was sharp with irritation, and following a crushed silence Grymes rose and walked to where his gear lay. He opened his blanketroll almost furtively, took a flask from its folds and uncapped it and drank deeply.

Grymes had not drawn a wholly sober breath in these two days on the trail, and by now Cody could think with certainty, *Yes sir, a conscience-killer for sure.* He had a fair idea why, remembering Trenna's conviction that Grymes had lied for Ames to cover up the real manner of Jared Gault's killing. Grymes, a simple man, was usually guided in his actions by a code of starkly defined ethics, and granted that Trenna was right, these had to be goading him fiercely. Idly Cody wondered whether Ed would finally crack and tell the Major the truth. Not that it would matter, if he knew Jeffrey Dembrow. Calem Gault, whether extenuated in the act or not, had killed the Major's son, and to that there could be only one answer.

The rising moon turned a face of bland serenity to the rocky scape, making indefinite patterns of outline and detail. The calm clear night and the cool unstirring air made Cody wonder if Sutter had been wrong about the storm. At this stage it would make no difference; the Major was bound to determined to write off the Gault brothers tonight and God's own wrath would not stop him.

Cody covered the thin smile that fluted his lips, by pulling a cigar from his vest pocket and clamping his teeth on it. He too had a man to kill, and getting his chance meant abetting that man's interests up to a point . . .

How would it be, putting a bullet into the one who, as far back as memory reached, had put the clothes on his back and the food in his belly? The thought was not pleasant, but since he hated the man, not intolerable either. Yet, weighing all things, even the self-admission that Trenna's direct solution was not entirely novel to his pattern of thinking, he knew that she herself had cinched the matter. Once Trenna was in a man's system, the drug of her blended into his feelings and thoughts till he could no longer separate them in his mind. Knowing what she wanted, he also knew against all misgiving what must be done.

Yet his deep streak of pessimistic caution made him scowl over an obvious dilemma. No matter how adroitly he handled it, the Major being struck down by an unknown hand would automatically open three avenues of speculation: accident, a Gault bullet finding its mark, or a possible motive among those in the Major's own party. If Cody, the next of kin, were in a too-convenient spot when the fatality occurred, no matter that nobody could prove a thing, the inevitable stain of suspicion would follow Trenna and him all their lives. Besides, he was no gunman.

Then hire one. The thought nudged him as he struck a match for his cigar so that he only stared at the match then, watching it burn down. Of course; hire a man for the job and make a foolproof alibi for himself. *But who?*

He let his gaze idle across the groups of crewmen, their rough, bearded faces sallowed by dancing firelight, giving each man in turn a brief or prolonged study. There were some tough hardcases in this lot, and all them were held by money and not by loyalty to Skull or the Major. A man had to care about his crew to inspire loyalty, and the Major did not. He paid gun wages for possible gun jobs—a man understood as much when he hired on.

He must choose his man with care, Cody knew; he could not discount the danger of a wagging tongue or some judicious blackmail later on. He needed a solid understanding in advance with the man he approached. His gaze touched Frenchy Duval and rested there.

The Cajun was sitting with four others, joking with them. His grin was white and startling in his dark-skinned face, a grin that had always made Cody think of a wolf baring its fangs. Perhaps Duval was no more than a human wolf; there were men like that, living for the next time they could savor the smell of blood, and an element of danger made it sweeter. Things had been fairly tame for Duval since his coming to Skull. *A long while between times for him*, Cody thought, and then: *Well, what do you care? He won't get cold hands and botch it.*

The savory odors of food and coffee were filling the still air, and the men began filing past the fire, filling their cups and loading their plates from the Dutch oven.

'You better get some rest, Uncle Jeff,' Cody drawled.

164

Jeffrey Dembrow was drinking coffee by the fire. He said, 'Rest,' and gave a hollow and bitter laugh. He pitched the rest of his coffee into the fire, gave a curt shake of his head as the cook held out a plate of food, then walked off a short distance to stare into the night.

Cody ate unhurriedly, and as he finished and stood, caught Duval's eye and tilted his head toward the shadows beyond the firelight where the spring was. Gathering up his few utensils, he tramped down to the water. He squatted, scoured his plate with sand and rinsed it in the murky water. Duval moved up beside him now, squatting to wash his own utensils. Not quite looking at him, Cody murmured, 'The Major will shake down a hornet's nest when he catches up with young Gault. Lead hornets. Can't say who might get stung.'

Duval's narrow shoulders shook to his silent chuckle. 'Ah yes, even the Major, eh? How long you and her take to come to this, eh?' He raised a hand swiftly. 'Soft, my friend; nothing to make the fuss on. Frenchy misses not a thing. It is my business to watch and know. The others, these clods, they guess nothing.'

Cody forced a smile. There was an obvious advantage to confiding in a man who had already guessed the truth. Shrewd and unscrupled, Duval had no cause but himself, and a habit of sniffing out every crosswind to that end. He also, Cody suspected, had an infinite talent for gauging how his assessments could be bent to his own use.

'You can see why the idea has me bothered, Frenchy,' he murmured. 'If an accident should happen to the Major and a man who stood to gain by it were close to him at the time, folks might wonder. A man has got to think of them things.'

'But yes, I understand this concern of yours well.' Duval delicately stroked a finger over his mustache. 'On the other hand, if a man who could not gain by this so-unlucky accident chanced to be close, nobody would think twice, eh? Still for being so close then, I think he too must gain. Ah, a great deal.'

'Whatever he wants, so long as I can stay sure of him. A man like that would know too much.'

Duval gave a small, expressive shrug. 'A man, even one like that, cannot stay on the move forever. The years cool the blood and give him an eye for the main chance. This oaf Grymes. Skull ranch deserves a better foreman.'

Again Cody's thin smile. Later Duval might find he wanted still more, but that could be dealt with in its good time. For now he had considered it a good bargain; Duval would make a useful and competent right hand when Cody came into his own at Skull. Being equally involved, they could trust each other absolutely.

'I couldn't agree more,' Cody said.

'Ah. And I wager that if you owned Skull you would replace him with a deserving man.'

'Why, I'm sure of it.'

'So am I.' Duval chuckled, his teeth a chalky glimmer in the dim light. 'So am I, my friend . . .'

CHAPTER FOURTEEN

Well after darkness had settled, Calem Gault and Ethan Jacks attacked the last impediment of earth and rock that barred the tunnel's end. Within the hour they had broken through, the loose surface soil collapsing into the tunnel and baring a ragged patch of cobalt sky.

There was no time to lose, for earlier they had spotted Cody Dembrow returning with the rest of the Skull crew. Now, with all of his men at his back, the Major would surely not delay another night.

Calem and Ethan returned to the shack, where Miss Charley had all the gear they would take packed and ready. Now she went ahead through the tunnel to fetch the two Gault horses from the little canyon back of the ridge where she had left them. Ethan, fussing like an old woman, told Calem to help his brother while he, Ethan, took care of a tag-end or two still hanging fire. Calem guessed that those tag-ends involved the Jacks' cache. Ethan's lifelong prospector's instinct, narrow and suspicious to the last, would not let him betray even a cache place that he would never use again, despite his self-proclaimed intent of turning over the store of gold to Calem.

Helping Jesse out of his bed, Calem assisted him into the mine passage. Jesse muttered between his teeth, 'Damn old miser,' as he edged gingerly along holding his game leg stiff.

Calem said nothing. He knew, from what both he and Ethan had deduced concerning Jesse's sly and abortive search for the gold, that his brother's leg was fairly mended. He was feigning the degree of lameness still hampering him, and Calem could only accept this knowledge with a bitter patience.

When they emerged on the far side of the ridge, and he had eased Jesse to the ground, Calem stretched his arms and tipped his face to the night sky, savoring the good taste of freedom after the days and nights in the confinement of the shack and tunnel. He noticed that a cool wind had dipped off the ridges. Masses of dense clouds were building darkly along the horizon and were scudding rapidly ahead of the wind; soon they would obscure the moon overhead. The air had a fretful and oppressive texture, forecasting the violence of the coming storm. It might have worked to Major Dembrow's advantage had they remained; now the reverse would be true.

Presently Ethan emerged from the tunnel toting his and Miss Charley's belongings. He dumped them to the ground, saying tersely, 'All right, Gault, you and me'll fetch yours out,' by which Calem knew that the gold had already been transferred to Ethan's person or possessions.

One trip back sufficed to bring out his and Jesse's things, along with a bait of grub that Ethan had thrown together. As they left the tunnel for the last time, Miss Charley appeared leading the two horses. In a few minutes they had gear and supplies cinched in place. With Jesse and the girl mounted on the horses, they left the ridge for a deep gulf of shadows that yawned below. By now the sable clouds were massing overhead and the moon was lost; but Ethan had no difficulty picking out his way across the stony scape, down black steep washes and around lofty spurs of rock. Calem guessed that he had mapped a back door through the broken ridges long ago, against any chance emergency.

It seemed a long time before they came onto a fairly regular belt of open slope, and Ethan took an easy way along its gentle grade. He opined that the rock-laced route they had just negotiated would throw off that breed tracker. Calem, walking beside him, silently doubted it; and then Ethan added, 'But that hellsmear of a storm that is building will wipe out our sign anyways.'

Glancing over his shoulder at Jesse and his daughter riding a good dozen paces to their rear, he lowered his voice. 'Got a bad feeling. That damn' brother o' yours. Listen. I hid gold in one o' your saddlebags.'

'Mine—'

'Shush your loud mouth,' Ethan hissed fiercely. 'Yours. Save me handing it over later—and with him looking on. He won't never guess you already got it unless you bray it out.'

Calem said with an uncomfortable lack of enthusiasm, 'You been calling my brother some hard things in front of the fact, old man.'

'All right, you wait on the fact,' Ethan said grimly. 'Just mind you don't give him your back meantime.'

On the heel of his words came a flat and not-distant boom, followed by a deep reverberation that trembled the earth. It had the kind of ground-quaking quality that sometimes came with nearby thunderclaps, but there had been no lightning.

Then Ethan grunted, 'Dynamite. He wants to make sure of us in the worst way. Means he will know shortly we're long gone.'

The first fat drops of rain began as they forged into the teeth of the wind, Ethan pointing them northeast toward the big canyon where they would lay up for as long as seemed necessary to throw Dembrow off the Gaults' trail. And now, as they struck across open country, the storm began in earnest. Calem and Jesse had their slickers and Ethan had fashioned a pair of canvas ponchos for himself and Miss Charley.

When they halted to don their waterproofing, Calem thrust his slicker at the girl, saying almost roughly, 'Here, you'll be better off in this. Swap you.'

'I don't need no favors.'

His jaw hardened. 'I am looking out for you from here on, and we might as well get straight on how it's to be. You wear this.'

Sitting horseback she stared down at him, her eyes squinted against the wind. 'I ain't your lookout. I never asked to be.' She spoke quietly, without the lashing anger he had expected.

'That don't make no difference.' He continued to hold out the slicker in his fist, and finally she took it and silently passed down the poncho.

The rain slashed in milky sheets against their bodies as they pressed on; despite the poncho Calem soon found himself soaked as the saturated air sent damp fingers probing to every dry inch of clothing and skin. Even in slickers, he knew, Jesse and the girl must be nearly as drenched. But the discomfort of cold and wetness was nothing to the welling relief of certainty that their tracks would be eradicated by the torrents of rain. Let Ethan have his brag of throwing off the pursuit;

Calem was only sure now of the throwoff. Held to a slow pace by two of them being afoot, they could be swiftly overtaken but for the rain. If the storm lasted only an hour longer, they would have covered enough distance to safely discount even the likelihood that by fanning out trackers Dembrow could pick up the trail when the rain had ceased.

After a while that earlier feeling of exultance passed off like the belly-glow from a shot of whiskey. The first windy plummets of rain ebbed into a steady downpour that it seemed would last forever. The unvarying buffet of drumming water through long hours of feeling out your way in a slate-colored oblivion of rainy darkness ate like a drug into your plodding body and mind, and the chill of a pounding wind taloned into your soaked carcass till your flesh went almost gratefully numb.

It must have been close to false dawn when the last pelting gusts slacked off and Ethan called a stop on high ground, close by a dense motte of young pine. Here they offsaddled and picketed the horses, then set to scouring up dead wood. The fire was built in a sheltered pocket girdled by trees and boulders, and with the dry heartwood from a deadfall they made it big and roaring, for all were half-frozen, their teeth chattering. They had wrapped any spare clothes in the ground tarps lashed with their soogans, and these had kept fairly dry.

While the girl slipped behind a rock with her small bundle, the men shed their wet clothes and changed quickly. Ethan said, 'We'll split the watch. You want to toss for the first?'

Calem shook his head. 'No, I'll take it.'

Jesse, who was spreading out his tarp and blankets, glanced at them. 'I'll sit up a spell.'

'I don't reckon you will,' Calem said. 'There's your leg. It'll want all the rest you can get.'

Their glances locked, and the hint of a smile grooved the wry corners of Jesse's mouth. *He knows*, Calem thought. *Let him sleep on it*. For his own part, he didn't think there would be much sleep tonight.

Ethan was not slow in yanking off his boots and rolling into his blankets, and he and Jesse were both asleep apparently at once. Calem spread out his tarp by a rock, wrapped himself in his blanket and settled his back to the rock, rifle across his outstretched legs.

Miss Charley returned to the fire and propped her wet dress, together with her long leggin-moccasins and an unmentionable or two, on sticks near the flames where the men's clothes were likewise placed. She had changed to another, but dryer, short-skirted dress; her legs and feet were bare, and the flames made a rosy smoothness of the pale flesh. He felt uncomfortably warm; he looked at the sky, then at the ground.

Leaving the fire, she came directly over to

him, making him look up. She was holding out the slicker. 'I'm obliged,' she said tonelessly, but there was a curious frown on her brow. Unhesitatingly she let the slicker fall, then dropped to her knees beside him, leaning fully into him as her face dipped to his. The young lips came hard into his; her mouth felt dry and awkward, but soon parted with a caressing succulence. The rifle fell aside unnoticed as his hands dropped to the skirt and felt the warm roundness of her flexed sturdy thighs, the hard smooth curves of her bare calves, while she knelt.

She promptly clouted him across the head, though not very hard, and came to her feet in a spare motion. 'That's all,' she said matter-of-factly. 'I was curious about something.' Going to where her blankets were, she spread them a proper distance from the fire, stretched out with a lazy, feline yawn, and covered herself. 'G'night. Keep a good watch.' She placed her back to him and tugged the blanket over her head.

Calem shook himself and picked up his rifle. The wild millrace of his heart had slowed, but his hands were still shaking. He felt dazed and stupid, and it was too late to ask what she had been curious about.

He had not intended to muse, since once he began wool-gathering sleep usually came quickly. But with Charley Jacks' hot sweet kiss still provoking the fantasies of warm

174

immediacy, he did muse. He soon dozed too, and the rifle slid groundward and his head bowed against his knees.

A savage, muffled curse shredded the mist around his brain; he came to confusedly, blinking against the fitful flamelight. It took him three full seconds to realize that Ethan and Jesse were tussling together on the ground, thrashing and grunting. Even as Calem lunged upright, he saw Jesse's fist, weighted by a pistol, rise and fall in two swift, down-clubbing blows. There was a single choking sound as if a man were reaching for his last breath; then Jesse rose, his lips peeling off his teeth as he swiveled around with the pistol leveled. But the muzzle had not come to bear on Calem when the latter's rifle froze him in place.

Calem said, 'Throw it away,' and Jesse, with a crooked smile, tossed the gun into the rocks.

Miss Charley had scrambled out of her blankets to reach the still form of her father. He was limp, with a crumpled waxen look, as she shook him, then laid her ear to his chest. 'There ain't no heart,' she whispered, turning a white face toward Calem. 'I think he is dead.'

Jesse's smile began to fade. 'Hell, he couldn't be.'

'You lay out flat and face down,' Calem said. 'Hands behind your head. Do it now.'

Jesse's eyes searched his brother's face; whatever he saw there made him obey without

175

more words. Only then, Calem moved to Ethan Jacks and stooped down to verify the girl's words.

'Jess. Where you hit him.'

'Hell, I rapped him on the chest once and on the jaw, was all,' Jesse said angrily. 'Let me look.'

Calem came very slowly to his feet, feeling the girl's intent eyes but not meeting them. 'That's wrong,' she said with a soft insistence. 'He can't be. I meant to tell him I was sorry for what I said before. I didn't mean that about leaving him. I got to tell him.'

Calem was looking at the handful of Ethan's belongings scattered around, his rucksack lying open where Jesse must have dropped it when Ethan had caught him rifling the contents. Looking at the girl, Calem shook his head. 'His heart was fixed to go any time. He told me himself. Never wanted you to know.'

She made a little throaty sound; she came around with the agility of a young animal, going after the rifle that lay by her tarp. Calem, expecting this, reached the weapon in time to pin it with his boot. She whirled to her feet, beating her fists against his chest and screaming, 'Just because he is your goddam brother!'

He did not argue; he barely hesitated before bringing his big fist around in a short sharp arc that ended behind her left ear. Without a sound she went limp. He caught her and lowered her to the ground, keeping his rifle awkwardly trained on Jesse.

'Get up,' he told him, and Jesse edged cautiously to his feet.

Oddly for one long moment another scene of long ago passed before Calem's mind's eye, not with the flickering uncertainty of most boyhood memories, but with the vividness of yesterday. On the night that their grandfather had died on the Missouri farmstead, the large brood of his children and grandchildren had been gathered weeping or silent at his bedside. And Aunt Willa had said softly, 'Now he's safe with Jesus.' It was Calem's mother, stung by grief too, who had said sharply, 'How do you know that, Willa? Because he was your paw?'

Martha Gault was a quiet farmwife, but now and again Calem had seen her rebel against the simple black-and-white judgments of her people. Of course Gramps had been a blasphemous, tippling old heathen to the very last, but Martha had not meant that; she had simply undercut the clannish conviction that your own kin were on the side of the angels no matter what. It was, as Calem had found, one of the hardest convictions to shake.

You could grow almost to manhood with a brother and bear witness to his all-around helling, even hear confirmation of it from his own lips, and still a part of you would not believe. For of all the people he knew, a man knew his kin the least, accepting only what he wished to concerning them.

Martha Gault had worn no blinders where her elder son was concerned; she had the gift of seeing the people she loved in a cruel white light and not loving them a jot less because of it. She had seen the irremediable drift of Jesse's whole life clearly, and had warned Calem at their parting. Now, fully understanding, he felt something die in him, hard and forever.

'I'm going to ride out of here,' Jesse said gently. 'You'll have to kill me to stop me, and you ain't got the guts for it.'

'Likely not. You'll ride out presently, all right.'

'You think you'll take me to trial, you mean. Think again.'

'No,' Calem said tonelessly. 'Not that. You'll ride out alone.'

Jesse's thin, jeering smile formed. 'So you'll turn me loose. I gave you credit for 'most no guts, and you got even less.'

'You could be right,' Calem conceded slowly. 'A man can't shoot his brother, or let someone else shoot him, or take him in to maybe get hanged. Law might not allow it was an accident, where I'd allow you that much. I am. There's still what you tried to do, rob a man, and him dead because of it.' He paused. 'What I aim to do, Jess, is bust you up in a way you'll never forget.'

'With what?' Jesse nodded at the rifle.

178

'You'll notch my ears and bust a couple kneecaps for me, huh?'

'No.' With a violent motion, Calem swung the rifle by the barrel, sailing it into the darkness.

Jesse's lips twitched with wicked amusement. 'You can't do it, Cal. This ain't no kid toe-the-line, and that's all you know. I learned more tricks than you ever thought of.'

'Watch yourself,' Calem said between his teeth, and shifted his body and moved in, squaring off. Jesse danced away, flicking a couple of jabs at his face, feinting to cover the sudden upswing of his foot in a vicious kick. Calem twisted so that it missed his groin, but found his thigh with a numbing impact. He staggered awkwardly in trying to follow Jesse's dancing form, and Jesse gave a low, confident laugh. He wove close in a tight, dodging pattern, feinted at Calem's belly and drew his guard low, then slashed at his face.

Calem felt gristle crunch in his nose; his eyes watered with red pain, and then Jesse's knee lifted into his belly. Calem pitched forward, bent with the agony of it, then floundered onto his hands and knees. He could not avoid Jesse's swinging boot as it met his jaw and flung him on his back. Calem's teeth met in his tongue-edge; he tasted the metallic hotness of pain and blood, and he rolled sidelong too late as a second kick caught him in the ribs. He gulped for breath and almost choked on it, toppling again on his back, and saw the raised boot descending to savage his face. He caught blindly and twisted with the strength of hurt and rage.

He heard the thud of Jesse's fall and the grunt of his driven breath; Calem rolled half-erect reaching dimly for sight; the saffron flicker of the crackling fire swam and caught steady. He and Jesse were on their feet at the same time. Calem rushed him and locked his arms in a brutal hug around Jesse's trunk, and felt him arch with the pain, gagging. He hooked a knee behind Calem's and threw his weight to bring them both down, at the same time trying to land atop him. Calem let his body twist with the fall, and Jesse was on the bottom as they struck. The impact, and Calem's tightening hold, crushed the breath from Jesse; he flailed both fists against his brother's neck. Calem ducked his head and doggedly took the pummeling, and put his full power into the hold, his shoulders bunching like a young bull's.

Jesse's body strung tight to his retching gurgle, and his blows became feeble pawings. *I could break his ribs*, Calem thought dimly, aware of a bitter mastery now, and slowly he relaxed his hold. He pulled back and got a knee under him, laboring for breath. Jesse writhed feebly, and the feebleness was part sham; abruptly his fist lashed out and caught Calem in the throat. Calem set his teeth and

180

came upright with Jesse's shirt doubled in his fist. Jesse's next panicked swing missed, but then he connected with a hard left that rocked Calem's jaw. He took the blows squarely, letting it fuel his anger afresh.

Spraddle-legged, he gave a brutal jerk that choked Jesse down to his knees, and twisted, watching the handsome face darken with congested blood as he vainly yanked at Calem's wrist. Now Calem drove his fist down in a full-armed smash, and then let go. Jesse slipped onto his side and rolled on his face; he braced his hands and pushed slowly to his feet. Reeling for balance, he spat blood and teeth; there was a mad glaze in the eyes that pounced on Ethan Jacks' rifle protruding from its saddle boot.

He made a diving lunge, landing on his belly and a half-doubled leg that happened to be his bad one. He shouted with the pain, but his hand closed over the gunstock and dragged the weapon free. He rolled quickly to his haunches in the same instant that he brought up the rifle, levering it.

Calem came swiftly in on him with two long steps, and as the second one took his full weight, brought his other leg up in a full-muscled sweep. His boot toe took Jesse directly under the right wrist as he worked the rifle; Calem heard the audible snap of bone breaking. Jesse's cry mingled with the roar of the rifle, as, angled upward by the kick, it discharged with the muzzle inches from Calem's sleeve. He winced with the bite of powderburn as the bullet grazed past his arm.

Jesse stumbled to his feet, his eyes wide and glassy, and Calem caught a handful of his hair and sledged a brutal hook into his jaw. Jesse fell against the trunk of a pine, his head rolling limply on his shoulders, and his knees started to fold. With an insensate lack of mercy Calem slashed a final blow at his bleeding face, and felt flesh tear; his fist skidded wetly off Jesse's face and crashed solidly against the tree. Pain splintered up his wrist and arm; he had dislocated a knuckle.

He kept his feet in the ragged pain of it, cuddling his hurt hand against his chest. Through eyes squinted nearly shut, he watched Jesse's sagging fall as he slipped down along the trunk to his knees, then pitched on his face.

Feeling his own legs starting to hinge, Calem dropped unsteadily to his haunches, his head hung and eyes shut, waiting for the pulsing hurt of his slipped knuckle to recede. He looked up at a sound, and saw Miss Charley sitting upright holding her jaw. Her eyes touched him with a steely puzzlement, then moved to Jesse who lay with his head turned. Her gaze widened on the wreck of his face.

'Sorry,' Calem said hollowly. 'I had to hit you. Couldn't have his blood on your hands.'

She said nothing, and he extended his injured hand, holding the index finger stiff. 'Grab that and pull hard.'

Mechanically she tugged. There was an instant of blazing pain that yanked a grunt from him as the knuckle was set. His whole hand throbbed with every beat of his heart, and it would be swollen like a balloon before long, he supposed. He would not be able to hold a gun with that hand, at least to fire, for days, and he did not want to think about that.

He crouched as he was, fighting the deep shock of various pains and gutted anger, while Miss Charley, at his direction, saddled Jesse's horse and tied on his gear. Afterward she stood watchfully by, her eyes hard and dry, as Calem awkwardly loaded his brother into the saddle. Jesse started to cant sideways, but caught himself; with his sound arm he struck Calem's bracing hand away. His right arm dangled uselessly with a broken wrist. He fisted the reins savagely, his bloody lips lifting off his broken teeth as he reached for words which came as a harsh whisper.

'I'm going to kill you for this, kid. Look sharp. I'll see you again.'

Coughing shallowly, he slowly turned the horse and, half-bent across his pommel, rode south into the wet bleak night.

183

CHAPTER FIFTEEN

Cody Dembrow was brought out of a blank, restless fog of sleep by the cook banging a ladle on a skillet. Sitting up in his blankets, he cursed under his breath as he rubbed a hand over the unshaven scrub of his jaw. The murky light presaging dawn was only now giving way to chill red streaks of sunrise on the distant peaks as the men, grumbling to wakefulness, stirred out of their soogans.

Cody sat on his soggy groundsheet and tugged on his boots. He swore again, aware of the strain that was building daily in him. He had a cold preconviction that even after last night's fiasco the Major would refuse to admit defeat, though it seemed that the Gaults had this time made certain their escape.

For Cody too the night's work had gone sour. In their brief talk by the spring, he and Duval had made a simple but explicit plan. When they rushed the hill, Duval would be somewhere at the Major's back. Watching for an opportunity after the shooting began, he would place his bullet, taking care to finish his man with one shot. Later the killing should not be greatly questioned, when during a heavy exchange of gunfire anybody's accidental slug might have done the work. And, since several men might die in the charge, the way of one man's death should not be scrutinized too closely so long as the onus of suspicion did not touch Cody, the one who stood to benefit.

That danger was already minimized since Cody would be atop the ridge setting the dynamite charge that would launch the attack. He had done so, arming himself with cartridges and detonators and a coil of fuse, then skirting around the ridge to ascend its flank. The Major had called out an ultimatum to the defenders, warning them that a refusal to surrender meant that dynamite would be used. When there was no answer from the darkened shack, Cody had applied detonator and fuse to a single cartridge and dropped it over the rim. It was sufficient to cave in a section of the mortared wall, and at once the Major and his men had swarmed up the hill.

But there was no shooting and no need to shoot. The interior was deserted, and in a few moments discovery of the mine tunnel and its extension to the far side furnished the explanation. The inmates had made good an escape, and the storm was already erasing whatever trail they might have left . . .

The men were shuffling past the Dutch oven, ladling food onto tin plates and filling their cups from the big cowcamp coffeepot. Cody had a belly full of moths this morning; he passed up the grub after the others had taken their helpings, but poured himself a cup of the hot black brew. As he hunkered by the fire sipping it, he let his narrowed gaze flicker to the Major who, pacing up and down, had touched neither food nor coffee.

Losing the Gaults so cleanly after coming within an ace of having them in his hands had been a blow, but it would not stop him from insensately pursuing his search, however hopelessly. They might spend days trying to pick up a fresh track.

Meantime Cody was faced with the unwelcome job of recasting his plan; he hadn't a notion of when or how a fresh chance might offer itself, and he could only shape his action to the opportunity.

Duval sidled up with his empty cup; he squatted by Cody and reached for the coffeepot, murmuring, 'What now, my friend, eh? You change the mind perhaps?'

'Not likely,' Cody said quietly. 'There'll be a right time, fella. Watch me and you'll know.'

Duval grunted and rose, moving away. Cody nursed his cup between his hands, brooding at the dawn-misted flats to the north. Thus he was the first to see the rider appear across a brow of ridge and come at a slow jog toward the camp. Cody threw out the dregs of his cup and came to his feet.

'Uncle Jeff.'

The Major came around on his heel as Cody pointed; he studied the steady approach of the rider, but gave no order. The men exchanged glances, then went on eating.

186

Within a couple of minutes the man was near enough to recognize. Cody frowned, unable to tell much except that he was slim and young and dark. His right arm hung limply as if from an injury, and his face looked as if he had lost a fracas with a meat-grinder.

Abel Sutter broke the silence meagerly. 'That there is Jesse Gault. I 'member him right enough.'

At once the Major's gun came up, the sound of its cocking brittle in the crisp morning air. Jesse Gault reined in a good ten yards off, lifting his hand palm out. He husked, 'You let that off before you hear me out and you could be damn sorry, mister.'

'I may take that chance,' the Major said with a peremptory snap. 'Unless you can explain why you were fool enough to ride into this camp.'

'In a minute.' Gault slung a leg over his pommel and dropped in a fluid motion from his stirrup to the ground. 'I need a cup of java first.'

'Get it then.'

Gault walked unhurriedly to the fire, bent and lifted the coffeepot. Cody, squatting close by, gave him a thoughtful study. There was no trace of swagger about Jesse Gault, only a latent feel of lobo meanness. Gault was the genuine article, Cody thought, a bad character of a seasoned toughness; a man learned to recognize that kind. He lacked his brother's

187

size, being slender and of average height and heft, with a lean, nervous tensile strength about him. His features were Calem's honed to a fine-chiseled sharpness, a handsome face now battered and drawn with pain and ugly with temper, particularly the eyes which held a chill arrogance that his beating must not have lessened. He wore no gun, Cody noticed, and his saddle boot was empty.

Gault filled a cup and drank half the near-boiling liquid, then said abruptly, 'Want my brother, don't you? I can tell you where he is. Better yet, take you there.'

The Major's answer was clipped and unhesitating. 'Why? You've helped him from the first, incidentally giving me a good deal of trouble. Why this about-face?'

'Look at this face. See this arm? That's why.'

The Major slightly lowered his pistol. 'Your brother did that? You've quarreled then.'

'Leave it at that.' Gault finished his coffee, flicked the dregs out and dropped the cup in one violent motion. 'I can take you to him.'

'I may find him without you. I owe you a debt too, Gault. I am tempted to collect it on the spot.'

'You won't, though.' Gault smiled, and the smile was not pleasant. 'You'll never find him without me, and you won't take the chance you can. He's the one pulled the trigger on your boy, not me, and he's the one you really want.'

'Very well,' the Major said coldly. 'My guarantee of your safety after you've told me his whereabouts—is that your price?'

'That's part.' Gault lifted his good hand, closing the fingers into a slow fist. 'The rest is, I want a gun and the first shot at him when you find him.'

The Major regarded him strangely. 'Why,' he said softly. 'You hate him more than I do.'

'You can give odds on it, pop.'

'My word, then. Out with it. Where is he?'

Gault told of the verdant canyon toward which Ethan Jacks had been leading them, and Abel Sutter put in then, 'I know the place, most of a day's ride from here. This Jacks was right enough if he said a man could live in that canyon for as long as he took a mind. Major, you would have plumb lost him there.'

The Major's eyes narrowed. 'You say that only the girl is now siding your brother, that Jacks is dead. How did he die?'

'He had him a bad heart.' Gault snapped his fingers. 'It went like that.' He moved his limp arm, wincing. 'Can anyone here set this wrist?'

The Major said nothing as he pursed his lips, staring at Gault, then he nodded in decision. 'All right, be ready to move out in five minutes. Take care of him, Sutter.'

While the grumbling men hurriedly finished breakfast, Abel Sutter set Gault's wrist with slender sticks for splints and tied it up. Without a word of thanks, Gault made a sling of his belt, then switched his dark look on Cody. 'How about that gun?'

'I got an extra,' Cody admitted, and got up and went to his gear, digging out his spare revolver.

Standing to one side like a withered wraith, Sutter said with a peculiar flatness, 'Who was it shot my horse?'

Gault smiled, and a vicious note thinned his voice. 'If it was me, old man, what you aim to do about it?'

The old tracker's eyes glinted ice-blue in his flayed-looking face. 'That's an answer,' he said meagerly, and walked noiselessly to where his saddle lay.

In a few minutes they rode out in a loose group, pointed northeast toward the high, rugged breaks below the deep folds of the near peaks. Sutter rode a steady lead, and the Major held behind him, heading up the others.

Quite suddenly Jeffrey Dembrow fell back beside Cody who was riding slightly to his left rear. He produced his fine cigar case and, to Cody's surprise, held it out. After a hesitation, Cody selected one of the tan Havanas and tucked it into his vest pocket.

'I'll save this.'

'Better if you'd get used to it.' The Major had placed a cigar in his mouth but did not light it; his manner was preoccupied, and presently he said, 'I've been meaning to talk to you for some time. No point putting it off.

190

You've thought, no doubt, that I've been unnecessarily hard on you, Cody. I have been, but not without a reason.' He took the cold cigar from his mouth, and Cody felt the touch of his iron-gray eyes. 'A man owes his blood something, Cody, and you and I have the same blood. I have never ignored that fact, even when Ames was alive; I had always intended to see that you would have your part in whatever I have built. Now that Ames is dead and you and I are the last Dembrows, the time has come to speak frankly.'

Cody said guardedly, 'I've never felt slighted, sir. You took me in and gave—'

'Yes, yes, all of that,' the Major waved his cigar with sharp impatience. 'I also worked you as hard as any common hand from the time you were ten, nor am I insensible to the humiliations you've endured at Ames' hands. Or of your working like a dog while he loafed. But Ames—Ames was my son. You understand that his rights were incontestable, while you had to prove yourself to me.' His stern voice softened a trifle. 'No man can help what he is born, Cody, but neither can a man evade the circumstances of his birth. The world will not have it otherwise, as cruel and unjust as that may seem. And because of what you were born, I needed to be sure—you had something to prove to me. Do you see?'

'I think so.' But Cody was not sure that he did, and in his shaken unease at this unexpected speech from a man for whom his ingrained hatred had become habit, he could feel only blank confusion.

'Well, you've weathered the storm in every way a man could hope. There'll be no more of this second-man role, Cody. You'll have to learn how to wear good clothes, how to order a good meal, how to smoke a good cigar.' He fumbled for a match, and Cody quickly struck one and held it to the Major's cigar—then lighted his own.

'Skull will be yours when I'm gone,' the Major went on. 'Of course Trenna will be provided for—a good-sized annuity and a home at Skull for a lifetime if she wants it.' He paused, puffing thoughtfully. 'A thought you might consider. Trenna is still a young and most desirable woman; I should think she'll marry again. And you'll be wanting a wife before long, Cody; you'll be well able to afford one now. It could work out very well for you both. After a decent interval, of course, and if she should prove agreeable.'

Cody could only manage to nod, and while they rode on in silence, his mind swam with a conflict of feelings. The Major always meant what he said, and the unshakable proof that he had made a complete and final acceptance of Cody was his candid suggestion concerning his son's widow. He had stepped quite literally into the place vacated by Ames.

The hour was still cool, but Cody found

192

himself sweating. Could he go through with what he had planned, after this? He must decide now, before they found Calem Gault and the golden chance was gone forever. Did the Major really think all the bitter years could be wiped out by one grandiose gesture? Could he really be that blind to the hatred that had cankered in his nephew for as long as he could remember?

But the deciding factor, when it came to Cody, came as certainly as death. By her own word Trenna would never wait for nature to take its course and the Major might live another twenty, even thirty, years. *She wants it all and she wants it now.* Then with a cold footnote of self-honesty: *And so do I, by God.*

CHAPTER SIXTEEN

Ethan Jacks had told Calem enough about the way to their destination so that, holding a course by the sun and bearing a few key landmarks in mind, he was confident of his direction. When, toward mid-morning, they angled onto a high, sage-stippled tableland, he knew that the canyon was close.

Now and then he gave the girl a worried look. She had said scarcely a word since they had buried her father; he did not like her dull silence or the frozen blankness that had

193

blunted the piquant vitality of her young face. The lively gamin of a girl he had gotten to know had gone; a stranger looked out of her eyes.

Her father's death had brought the change, but how deep it went he did not know. He did have a fair idea that in some obscure way she was blaming herself because the last intimate words that had passed between Ethan and her were bitter ones. That was as wrong as could be, he thought, but he sensed too that for the time he could say or do nothing that would help.

He put his attention solidly to the business of getting them to the canyon that now, according to all signs, should be just ahead. They left the tableland and crossed one timber-shaggy hill and then another, where they angled onto a dim game trail.

The discovery quickened his pulse, for this had to be the trail which Ethan had said would, if traced north for a few hundred yards, lead them directly down into the canyon.

They followed it onto a gently tilting bench where giant fir flourished and only a fine mottling of sunlight touched the needle-fall ground. The parklike area was nearly free of underbrush, and the trail switchbacked indifferently around treeboles and other obstructions. They came to a frothing creek which cut steeply through the bench and forced the trail to a right-angled turn along its bank. They had followed the water-course only a brief distance when the bench terminated in a gradual fallaway of land that was the first dip into the canyon. The game trail followed the creek as it poured into the gulf, and unhesitating, Calem led off down it, he afoot and Miss Charley on the horse.

As the dip steepened, Calem had a clear view of the canyon floor, and it took his breath away. The gorge was bottlenecked at this end, but beyond that it grew to a width of several hundred yards, and he could not see the far end. The soaring, almost vertical walls were crowned by beetling overhangs, and sunlight colored the upper heights of sandstone and limestone with waterstain streaks of iron and salt. The racing stream sparkled over vivid rocks and chattered here and there into short rapids. The dip choked to a narrow slit, and the dense young fir climbing its flanks were bark-wet from the rise of pearly mist. This laid a clean, odorous sweetness in the air, and his senses absorbed it pleasurably. As they neared the bottom, the stream spilled into a creaming gush of rainbow-veiled falls, and they put the horses carefully down its rocky bank and tackled the last descent to where it ended in an overgrown outwash fan.

From above Calem had seen that the canyon floor was mostly lush, open meadows laced by timber mottes. Now he saw that the grass was deep and luxuriant and, because the rising sun was only now wiping back the shadows in this cliff-girdled cleft, glistening with dew which shook down to their passage.

He took the lead, forgetful of everything else in his burning eagerness to explore this pocket paradise. The stream wound away downcanyon, now and again losing itself in thick stands of cottonwood, box elder and ash, and it was fed at various points from springs or by trickles from the upper heights. Sometimes it eddied into deep still pools, and where there were shelving rocks he watched for trout. Once he spotted the granddaddy of them all, thick as a man's calf and longer than his arm, fin-batting against the streambed gravel. Stopping to listen, he found the brooding, awesome stillness and solitude broken only by a hum of bees and a soughing of wind from upcanyon.

Calem's first excitement was crystallizing into a vague form now, and he worked back and forth in erratic zigzags, studying the sunswept lay of meadow and timber with a practical eye. As well as plentiful grass, he took note of sheep-fat and antelope bush and other plants fine for stockfeed. Under the rim hard by the west end, he came on a steep notch in the cliffs that was almost obscured by clotting thickets. He rode partway into it, breaking brush, and found that it widened suddenly into a broad pass that led north across fairly regular terrain. The brush could be cleared, and a well-laid charge at this shallow ridge or that narrow passage would slough away enough rock to make an easy trail . . .

Back in the big canyon he studied with more care a site he had idly reconnoitered, close to one flank but well out of danger of falling rimrock. A tight log house here would be cool in summer, warm in winter, with a fine view of the creek and the lower canyon. Almost before he realized what he was doing, he had picked up a sharp-stick, preparatory to marking off the dimensions of a cabin.

Then, with a wry grin at his own thoughtless fervor, he dropped the stick from a hand that was almost too swollen to hold it. He could move the recently disjointed finger with a little effort, but it hurt like the devil; he had torn cartilage, and he would have to manage left-handed for days.

Kneeling by the streambank, he plunged his throbbing hand into the chilly waters, letting go a sigh at the instant relief. Almost guiltily he glanced at Miss Charley whom he had almost forgotten. She stood by the horse, fingering the reins. She had apathetically followed his exploration without question, and her expression was an incurious blank.

'Been woolgathering,' he said lamely, making a circling gesture. 'Got thinking how a man might settle smack here in the canyon and run a few head. Providing he set his sights in a modest way, he could make out fine. Plenty of

197

big timber for building, plenty game for that trail, trout in the crick, and a man could scratch out a truck patch and pack in suchlike few things as salt and flour and sugar he would need. Grass and water to suit, and no want for riders on drift lines with just a few cattle inside these cliffs. No pocket, brush or potholes for them to get boxed or hung up in.'

From him this was a whole lot of talk, and it had the effect of getting the girl's half-attention; she stirred her shoulders and looked around. She said without much interest, 'How you going to get cows in and out of this?'

'That little side pass. A few charges of giant powder choicely laid would open her up. You could haze out a batch of growed stuff now and then and drive to Mercyville, which has got a railroad.'

She gave a small indifferent nod and he frowned, thinking, *It is time we cleared the air.* 'Sorry I had to hit you back there. Couldn't let you kill him. It ain't only he's my brother. Killing your pa wasn't his intent. He couldn't of knowed about your pa's heart.'

'Neither did I,' she said in a dull voice. 'He never told me. He could of told me that and things would of been different; I wouldn't of said I was leaving him then. Why didn't he tell me?'

'He didn't know how, I reckon.' Calem stood up, gingerly drying his hand on his shirt. 'It surely wasn't because he hadn't a feeling for

198

you. All the gold he took out was meant for you. He told me so, but he never knew how to say it.'

She raised eyes, narrow with disbelief. 'Why would he tell you that?'

'Because he wanted me to see after you when he went. He would have left us after we reached this canyon. He didn't figure to burden you none.'

'That makes it all the worse.' She turned, pressing her face against the horse's mane. 'I pushed him clean out of my life at the last.'

'Look here,' he said brusquely, coming over to her. 'Look at me now. You want to start setting blame, blame me ahead of anyone. If I hadn't got Major Dembrow after me, we wouldn't have found you. Or say you're the one found us—if you hadn't, your pa might have died then pinned like he was. You want to go way back, if he hadn't took that bullet next to his heart first place, a little thump on the chest wouldn't of finished him.' He frowned, trying to form the gist of the idea. 'Miss Charley, a body just can't hold himself to account for what he didn't know. So don't you.'

She raised her face, but said nothing as she plucked absently at the horse's mane; finally she shrugged. 'Whatever the cause, it don't matter now. He is gone, and all the talk won't change that. If he needed me, he was the only one who did.'

'I need you.' The words left him without hesitation or thought; even when he realized what he had said, there was nothing to think about. He had stated a simple truth, surely and instinctively, and he only wondered at his slowness till now in grasping it.

He watched her eyes, seeing for a moment something besides the dullness of despair. But then she shook her head. 'I reckon not. Sure is nice of you to say so, though.'

'I ain't just saying it,' he said angrily. 'But I surely don't know how to make you see it, that's plain.'

Again the hint of tentative aliveness quickened her smooth expression, though her voice was doubtful. 'Maybe you better just say it, Gault.'

'Well.' He ducked his head and rubbed his neck, digging his heel at the ground. Finally he arced a hand about him. 'This place is made to suit for someone who don't fancy town living or town ways.' That much of what he meant to say came easily enough. He had really made the decision, if unconsciously, at first sight of this canyon; a man took such a feeling deep into his bones where it became a part of him. 'I feel mighty strong on this canyon.'

'Sure is pretty here,' she said without expression; she was giving him no help.

'It won't be nothing without you.'

'We got to stand front of a preacher.'

'Well, sure,' he said stiffly. 'What did you

think?'

'You got a ring or something to pledge me?' He shook his head and she came to him, raised on her toes and kissed him solemnly. 'That'll do for a pledge. No, you keep your big hands to yourself. I like them is the trouble, a sight too well. We'll just wait.'

That would be for a while, he judged dourly, as he intended remaining in the canyon until he could be reasonably sure that Dembrow had given up the search. The time would not be wasted; he could fell and trim logs for their future home with Ethan's hand-ax and perhaps get a start on the actual building. Later they could get what carpentry tools they needed from Mercyville.

But he wanted to set up immediate camp elsewhere in the canyon, with an eye to security. The chance of anyone coming here might be practically nil, but he was taking no chances. He had reconnoitered enough of the canyon to ascertain the ideal site for their temporary bivouac. A giant chunk of the rimrock had collapsed long ago, forming a low ridge of massive rubble at the base of the north wall. Now overgrown by thick brush and scraggly young firs, it seemed made to order. The brush would lend good concealment, and from the slight elevation they could command a fair view of much of the canyon, including the descending trail at its mouth. At least they would spot anybody coming into the canyon before being seen themselves.

They moved onto the rise and began to ready the camp. With the hand-ax Calem slashed down some saplings and fashioned a pair of half-shelters for them, using his catch-rope to lash the poles together and thatching each with leafy slashings.

Deep in the afternoon he was dozing on his blankets flung over a springy bed of boughs, hat tipped over his eyes. Miss Charley aroused him with a vigorous shake. 'I seen something on the rim, so I looked with them glasses of yours. Here.'

Calem took the fieldglasses from her hand and trained them on the canyon terminus where the trail was, at once catching the colored stipples that were men and horses moving downward through the black-green of heavy foliage that almost masked the long descent.

He was aware of Miss Charley's intent gaze on him, and now she said quietly, 'Them, huh? Couldn't be nobody else.'

Calem lowered the glasses; he tasted the stunning acceptance of what his eyes verified, and yet, not wanting to believe it, could not begin to grope for the why or how of Dembrow being able to follow them here.

The canyon that should have been a refuge had become a trap; it formed a sheer-walled cul-de-sac at this end, and the one brush-grown defile which he had marked earlier as an ingress-egress for cattle was very near the other end where Dembrow's party already was. In any case, an ex-military careerist like Dembrow would have any potential escape routes spotted and covered within minutes; common sense told Calem that much, and he promptly discarded the idea of escape.

He also realized, with a terrifying sense of discovery, that he could find in him no real wish to run any more. His first reaction had been the feel of overwhelming hopelessness that keens into despair; if against all odds Dembrow could somehow track him here, what was the use of trying any more? Yet already that feeling had ebbed into a wolfish determination.

Live or die, he was through running. It made his next move easy to decide. What his mind—or that part of it which housed the God-fearing conscience of Calem Gault— shrank from was not fear, but the utter ease with which decision came.

Somehow he must kill Major Jeffrey Dembrow.

It was another chilling glance into the submerged brute that was the essential man, bringing home to him with a shocking insight the truth that he was finally, at bottom, of the same stuff that he hated in other men; he found a kinship in Jesse's amoral instincts and in Dembrow's rapacity. And he knew with equal certainty that, if he survived today to resume the ingrained patterns of his thoughts and ways, this moment, this insight, would always stay vividly with him . . .

Miss Charley's gaze held steady on his face. 'Same as before,' she said softly. 'We got us a wall at our backs.'

Calem lifted his eyes to the rimrock above them, and he shook his head. Not quite the same, as soon as Dembrow thought of sending men to circle onto the rim and fire down on them. And sooner or later he would, if he could not take them from the front. The chance that he could not was good, for the dense screening of brush and rocks on this shallow rise might enable two people to hold off men who would have to cross a bare slope to reach them. Only the advantage would be a short-lived one.

'My gramps—he was a mountain man— used to say when you're attacked by Injuns, shoot the leader first. May stop the rest.'

Miss Charley nodded her calm understanding. 'You reckon to get you a leader?'

'Best chance I see of that is finding him before he finds us.'

He told her what he had in mind, and she nodded with a grave reluctance. 'I don't like it much, but two of us can maybe bring her off.'

'You stay here where they won't find you,' he said flatly. 'And I don't want no argument about it.'

CHAPTER SEVENTEEN

With a last well-stressed admonition to the girl to stay where she was and lie low, Calem came off the short slope at a loping run. He plunged into the overgrowth of young firs that began just below the rise, and worked up-canyon.

He had no definite plan beyond lining up Jeffrey Dembrow in his gunsights. That meant getting dangerously close to his man, for with his injured right hand he could not handle a rifle; the best he could do was manage his old Walker pistol with an awkward and unpracticed left hand.

He moved at a swift trot where the forest was free of underbrush, and where it was not, broke brush with a heedless impatience. He kept as much as possible to the concealing timber, leaving it only where the trees thinned into grassy stretches, quickly crossing these. Only when he was quite close to the head of the canyon did he slow and make his way carefully. Here on the lower canyon floor he could not see the oncoming riders, but they must be close now, and they would be cautious in their approach.

Calem came to a break in the timber where, by dropping prone behind a deadfall, he had a concealed view of the stream and the old game trail that meandered along its bank—the likely approach for a man working downcanyon. He slipped out his Walker and braced the muzzle across the deadfall's mossy trunk, squinting down the long blued barrel. He judged that with a steady eye and a firm hand he could kill a man at the closest point on the trail, where the stream made a deep curve this way. Then he would fade with all haste into the timber and hope the Skull crew, shorn of leadership, would give up. A forlorn hope perhaps, but his only one.

He waited, his heart thudding against the earth. The first inkling he had that his idea had gone awry was when two men, moving at a low crouch, came afoot into sight through a gap in the timber beyond the stream; they were quickly swallowed again by the trees. Then a crackle of brush somewhere at his back alerted him to other men working through this same timber. He waited tensely, but the sounds faded away as the men went on past, missing him by many yards.

The Major plainly had no intention of riding boldly into a possible ambush; he had split his men into small parties that were flung out and infiltrating gradually downcanyon, covering and searching a good deal of ground as they went.

But where was the Major himself? Even if he knew, evading the small group of Dembrow's men to get near him would be a ticklish job. Now he heard more men on foot entering the motte where he was laid up; his spine crawled unpleasantly at their nearness this time. Rather than lay up here till he was found, why not boldly hit the open and continue his search for the Major?

He gathered himself and made a short run across the open; he made the high stream bank and slid down it on his haunches to water's edge, crouching there while he scanned up and downstream for a shallow fording. Then the muttered voices of men moving his way reached him. Lifting his eyes till they barely topped the bank, he saw two of them come into sight of the trail upstream. They would be on him within a minute, and caught between the streambanks, he couldn't break for cover without being seen. There was only one thing to do, and Calem did it. Jamming his gun under a matting of grass, he slid almost noiselessly into the water, letting it close over him neck-deep like an icy cloak.

The wicked chill of the high country stream wracked him to the bones as he waited; when the voices of the men were almost above him, he submerged his head completely. Peering up through the water he saw the men's refracted images pass by along the trail. When his lungs seemed ready to burst with stale air, he lifted his head barely above the water, hugging the bank.

The pair had halted a ways downstream to converse, he knew from the low-pitched voices. Their words barely reached him, but he recognized them as Cody Dembrow and Frenchy Duval.

' . . . and locate the Major,' Cody was saying quietly. 'We'll split up here. I got to be with Grymes or some of the others when it happens.'

'You are sure the Major he went that way, eh?'

'Dead sure, and he was by himself. Ed Grymes and a couple others were scouting in that direction too; watch out for them. There won't be another chance like this, Frenchy, so get going.'

There was no more talk, and now Calem dared raise his head enough to see that the two of them had parted company, Cody moving on downstream while Duval cut at right angles into the trees. Though making little sense of what he had heard, Calem had gleaned one solid fact: follow Frenchy Duval and ·he would find Jeffrey Dembrow. He left the water and scaled the bank. Pausing only to retrieve his pistol from the grass, he started into the timber after Duval.

The gunman was stalking through the trees like a gaunt wolf; Calem stayed well to his rear, just in sight of him. There was something amiss here, dovetailing with the cryptic speech that had passed between Duval and Cody, but that troubling notion was only a vague undercurrent below Calem's own burning preoccupation.

Duval had neared the canyon's north wall when he pulled to a stop at the fringe of a clearing. For a moment he was stiff and intent, and then he swung aside. He glided along behind the thickets that hedged the clearing and was quickly lost to sight. Calem halted uncertainly, but then moved up beside the clearing. He gave the humpy, rock-strewn meadow one quick glance, then dropped down on his haunches to avoid being seen. The stocky form of Major Jeffrey Dembrow was plodding at a dogged, tired walk across the meadow. He was almost at its center, not twenty yards away, and he was a clear target.

Calem fingered the long pistol laid across his knees, but did not raise the weapon. In this moment the troubling fact of Duval's stealthy circumnavigation of the clearing, shifted to the forefront of his mind, and suddenly he understood. Duval's behavior matched his own, which meant that Duval was here for the same reason. The gunman was circling behind the thickets only to select the choicest spot from which to fire a deadfall shot. *But at the Major?*

The answer to his disbelief came in the high crack of a rifle from the brush some yards away.

Calem heard the audible grunt of the breath smashed from Jeffrey Dembrow's body as the slug's impact drove him head foremost in a stumbling fall. He rolled over once, pawing feebly for his fallen rifle, and got it. His rollover had carried him onto his belly and face behind a low outcrop of crumbling rock. Weakly he levered the rifle as another shot sang off the outcrop.

The man who had ruthlessly dogged his trail was pinned and helpless and probably dying, but Calem's taste of bitter satisfaction was brief. If Dembrow were killed by the Cajun, and Calem were the only witness, he would be blamed for a murder he had not committed. *Maybe that's what they want!*

Simultaneously he realized how a swift bold gamble might twist this situation to his advantage. At this point he had almost nothing to lose, and with that thought he made his move.

He broke into the open, running low and hard toward a deep-worn gully that cut across the stony meadow. He covered these few yards braced for a bullet at each straining step. But none came, and he hit the raw cutbank and skidded down it on his back and crouched at the bottom, panting. Duval must have been too surprised or puzzled by his action to fire.

Calem scrambled on his hands and knees along the crooked pebble bed of the dry wash, working deep into the clearing. He had taken note of a bend which angled close to the Major where he lay sprawled behind the outcrop. Reaching the bend, Calem raised himself by careful degrees until he could see the wounded man lying with his legs pointed toward the gully. A great crimson stain had spread across the soiled back of his linen shirt, and his rifle lay slack in his hands; his head had slumped onto one bent arm, and he was unconscious, Calem saw.

He clambered from the wash and, flopping on his belly, crawled to the Major's side. Instantly Duval laid down a quick close fire that chipped splinters from the outcrop; his angle of fire was poor. Tugging and rolling the Major's inert slack body with him, Calem worked back to the lip of the cutbank. Two of Duval's bullets kicked dirt against his legs before he pushed the Major over the bank and then followed him.

Now, with the two of them cut off entirely from Duval's fire, Calem lay for a moment regaining his breath. He heard an abrupt outbreak of shots from the east, and had the sickening thought that some of the Skull men had found, and tried to reconnoiter, the rise where Miss Charley was hidden, only to be met by her rifle. *They don't know it's her and not me shooting.*

If only Duval's shots would pull a few of them back here. Able to handle only a pistol, Calem could not match the Cajun's fire.

Again cautiously lifting himself, gun in hand, he scanned the irregular hedge of thickets that bounded the south side of the meadow. He gave a rigid attention to the place where the smudges of powdersmoke had betrayed Duval's hidden gun, alert to any telltale sound or movement.

The groin-knotting seconds passed into long minutes. Calem's hand ached around his gun and a wash of sweat stung his eyes. Leaning his chest against the cutbank, he carefully wiped the sweat away, using his injured hand. He was far past fear, but he wondered how long a man could live with the sheer gut-deep weariness that no longer seemed to ever leave him for very long . . . *where was Duval?*

He has to be up to something. All you can do is wait and hope you see what is coming before it happens.

Now the noise of hurried voices and the breaking of brush indicated that the Skull men were coming on the run, drawn by Duval's shots. Calem felt almost a relief, though he could not be sure that even his having aided the Major would improve his situation. They were coming from the east toward his back, so Calem pushed wearily away from the west bank to face the opposite way.

Even as he started to turn, he caught a whisper of quick steps across bare earth. He stopped in mid-movement, trying to isolate that sound from the distant commotion made by the approaching Skull crew.

So suddenly that he was taken wholly by surprise, Frenchy Duval stepped into sight from around the sharp bend down the gully.

His steps were lithe and stealthy; his gun was held ready. Calem was already half-facing that way, and now recovering, he finished his turn in a desperate haste as he brought up his gun. His heel turned against a rock and his wild clawing for balance upset him entirely; falling, he landed close to Jeffrey Dembrow's limp body.

The sudden drop saved him as Duval's bullet smashed into the raw earth of the bank above him. Sprawled on his side facing the Cajun, Calem had no conscious thought of his gun being pointed. Yet it was, and he shot in a kind of reflex.

The high-angling bullet took Duval under the jaw and wrenched his head on his neck with almost the snapping force of a hangman's noose. He turned like a toe dancer, his body still arched from the shot, and toppled face first against the gully bank. The tension left his body and he slipped down in a sidelong roll. His arms straightened and twitched.

It had been a neat ruse, Calem thought. While he had riveted his attention on the spot where the gunman had last fired, Duval had swiftly slipped back through the timber, and come onto the meadow at Calem's back. Dropping into the gully as Calem himself had done, Duval had come up quickly on his blind side. Luckily Calem had turned then.

He stepped over to Duval and picked up his pistol. Despite an ugly head wound, the Cajun might still be dangerous.

213

Major Dembrow groaned and stirred, but Calem gave him only a scant glance. By now the Skull men were in sight, starting across the meadow. Ed Grymes lumbered in the lead, and he boomed an order for them to fan out.

Calem shot into the air then, lifted his voice in a shout: 'Mr. Grymes, don't come any closer. This here is Gault. I got the Major with me. You come after me, he will get the first bullet that's fired.'

Grymes came to a dead stop, raising a thick arm to halt the others. 'How we know you got him?'

Calem hesitated, then bent and scooped up the Major's fawn-colored Stetson and waved it high. 'See this?'

'I see it. Could mean he is already dead.'

'No, he is hurt. But he'll be dead soon enough without you keep your distance.'

Grymes growled, 'What do you want, kid?'

'Ten minutes. I need to talk with the Major. He has got to hear me out.'

Belatedly he remembered that Grymes, who had lied about the way of his father's killing, had every reason for allowing him no time to persuade the Major otherwise. He braced himself, half-expecting Grymes to give the order at once to charge the gully.

Surprisingly, Grymes only nodded, saying gruffly, 'Ten minutes. Then it's root hog or die for you, Gault. All right, boys, pull back to the trees.'

214

Calem glanced over at the Major who was flat on his back, his eyes wide open and focused on Calem now. Grunting, Dembrow fumbled for the pistol still holstered at his belt. Calem dropped to one knee beside him, drew the weapon and tossed it out of reach.

The Major's one eye held bitter fire; he whispered, 'Finish the job. That is more your style.'

Calem dug out his bandanna. 'I ain't the man who shot you.'

'As you didn't shoot my boy?'

Calem motioned at Duval's crumbled body. 'That's your man. I dragged you into the gully after he shot you.'

The Major's lips twisted as if on the edge of acid denial; then his eyes clouded as his gaze touched Calem's hand, swollen and discolored. His gaze flicked back to Duval, and he said abruptly, 'Where is your rifle?'

'Left it behind. I can't hold one.'

'No, I shouldn't think so,' the Major said softly. 'It was a rifle that fired at me. Frenchy was carrying one, but where is it?'

Calem, occupied with stanching the flow of blood as best he could, gave a shrug. 'Likely you'd find it back in the bushes where he shot at you. It would of just been in his way when he sneaked up on my back.'

'But you got him?'

'Yes, sir,' Calem rocked back on his heels. 'Major Dembrow, I want you to listen.'

Dembrow gave a savage shake of his head. 'I don't understand this, Gault. I don't understand you. Why help me?'

'To save my neck,' Calem said coldly. 'I could of killed you myself. Maybe I will be sorry I didn't. But I wanted to handle this another way bad enough to take a chance.'

'Chance?'

'That you will listen to me once. I told the truth about how your son gunned my pa, whether or not you want to believe it.'

Jeffrey Dembrow held a hand tightly over his right chest where the bullet had emerged; sweat stood on his forehead and his whiskered jaw was ridged with pain. 'Boy, that is saying that Ed Grymes lied under oath. You expect me to believe that of a man who has been loyal to me twenty and more years?'

'Loyal or not,' Calem said stubbornly, 'it happened the way I said.'

The Major watched him through half-shuttered eyes. His stern face was masked against any betrayal of pain, but did not quite wall off his self-struggle with the unrelenting obsession that had driven him for days. 'It was a fair fight with Ames,' he muttered. 'He was my son and you killed him—but even so.'

'Yes, sir. It was fair. I went after him for sure, but I had a strong reason.'

'I am thinking of two things,' the Major went on; he grimaced with a twinge of pain, and his voice sank to a whisper. 'First that your action in helping me was not that of a moral weakling, as which I would designate a liar, under oath or otherwise. Also you have given me back a life, my own, for the one you took, my boy's. I cannot ignore these things. I will give you a fair hearing. Was that Ed Grymes you called to before?'

'Yes, sir.'

'Hail him again; say that I want to see him.'

Standing, Calem cupped his hands to his mouth and called to Grymes. When the foreman's deep-throated answer came, Calem shouted, 'The Major says come over here, but let me see you throw away your guns first.'

He expected at least a token objection from Grymes, but again the man surprised him. Without a word Grymes stepped into plain view, and discarded both his rifle and handgun. He plodded across the meadow holding his hands out from his body, and reaching the gully, made a clumsy descent of the cutbank. His startled look shuttled from the Major to Frenchy Duval, and back again.

'Duval tried to kill me,' the Major whispered. 'Young Gault saved my life. We'll attend to the wherefores of that matter later. Just now I want you to tell me again how Jared Gault died. Exactly as it happened, Ed.'

Ed Grymes' head dropped till his chin touched his chest. He cleared his throat gently. 'Major, that hurt of yours should be looked to proper.' His deep voice trailed and he sighed, lifting his eyes. 'I reckon it had to come out. I tried drinking it away, but that ain't no good. Ames lied, Major, and so did I. Gault never had a chance. It happened the way the boy here told it.'

'In the name of God,' the Major breathed. A deeper pain than any that was physical roiled in his face. 'Why?'

'Ames said if I wanted to keep my place at Skull I would toe the line like he wanted.'

A shadow fell across the dry streambed, bringing Calem's gaze around and up. Cody Dembrow stood above the cut-bank, a gun in his fist; he said tightly, 'Throw it down, boy.'

Calem let his gun thud to the ground, feeling a dour disgust for his carelessness. Cody had come alone, but had he crossed the meadow with the whole crew, Calem would have been too absorbed by Grymes' confession to have noticed.

Cody dropped to the bottom of the gully, at once swiveling a sharp glance on the prone form of Duval. The gunman's eyes were closed; his hands were clutched to his chest and his breath was a stertorous sigh.

'You can put that up, Cody,' the Major said tersely. 'Duval shot me. It was Gault who prevented him from finishing the job.'

'Frenchy?' Cody's face held a thoroughly bland amazement. 'Why you reckon for?'

Of course he wanted to tell the Major of the intrigue between Cody and Duval, but Calem

218

let the impulse die. Jeffrey Dembrow's sense of fair play was already restraining incredulity on a fine leash where Calem Gault was concerned. And Cody, who had not put his gun away but only lowered it, might react unpleasantly.

'That will keep,' the Major said. 'I want to hear Ed out. Ed, you might have told me the truth after Ames was dead. Why didn't you?'

'I was as skeered of how you would take it.' Grymes' massive shoulders lifted and fell. 'I can't live with it no more. Now it's out, anyways.'

'Cody,' the Major husked. 'You and Ames spoke together just before his death. Did he confide in you at all about the Gault killing—anything—?'

Cody started visibly; he was caught off-guard, kneading his lips between his teeth as he watched Duval through narrowed eyes. Though the breath was rattling in Duval's throat, he was still alive, and Calem thought. *He might have enough left to talk some yet. Wonder what it is between them?*

Cody said, 'No, sir. Nothing.'

The Major nodded as if in a trance, his eyes strangely dead. 'As you say, Ed, now it's out, all of it. Your blame, Ed—and mine.' He grimaced again as pain shook him. 'Not only this, not only what I've done to you, Calem Gault, or even what my boy did to your father. Started long before that. All signs plain for a long time ... never let myself see 'em because ... didn't want to. Ames ... bad ... he was bad ... my doing ...'

Grymes said urgently, 'Major,' but Jeffrey Dembrow's eyes had closed and he gave no response.

'Ah, what a pity,' came Duval's quiet croak. He had pulled himself partly erect, his back to the cutbank; he coughed as the effort of speech brought more blood pumping from his throat. 'He did not have the time to ask you about why I shoot him, my friend, eh?'

Cody's nostrils flared as his gun, held in his hand by his side, began to arc up. Duval's hand, lax on his thigh, rose with a sunglint racing along metal. The double-barreled pocket pistol almost concealed in his fist blasted twice.

Cody stumbled as one bullet, then the other, took him within a two-inch-wide circle above the heart. The second shot knocked him backward, but he could never have known when he hit the ground.

CHAPTER EIGHTEEN

Duval thought he was dying, and in the next few minutes he told enough to bring some sense out of his scheme with Cody. Assassinating the Major, he said, had been an

220

idea hatched by Ames Dembrow's young widow in collusion with Cody. By this time the whole crew was gathered in the gully around the two wounded men and the dead one, all of them listening in still-faced silence to Duval's explanation.

To Calem's question, one of them dourly reassured him that Miss Charley was unhurt; in fact all of the men had withheld their fire on realizing that it was the girl alone, not Calem, doing the shooting. Her rifle was still making it warm for them when, hearing the continuing gunfire from this direction, they had headed back upcanyon.

Abel Sutter had finished his examination and dressing of the unconscious Major's wound, and now he announced that Dembrow would be fiddle-fit with a proper herb poultice, for which he had seen the makings hereabouts. Then Sutter turned his attention to Duval, after a minute remarking, 'Lead missed yer backbone an' big vein clean's a whistle. Allus had the feeling you was born to hang.' Sutter lifted his blue-bright eyes to Calem then, saying inscrutably, 'Seen your brother yet?'

Calem frowned, uncomprehending. 'What do you mean?'

'He's about. He come into camp this mornin' and told the Major where you was. Come here with us. He is in a powerful sweat to see you decked out for six foot of earth.'

Calem felt the bone-deep shock of

realization; he should have seen at once that Dembrow could never have found the canyon by chance, that Jesse's savage venom would carry him this far. Beaten and brutally marked, Jesse would do anything to salvage his wild pride; stripped of only that much, he would be nothing.

Calem passed a narrow-eyed glance across the still faces of the crew, then mechanically gave the surrounding timber a wary scrutiny. If Jesse were not present, he had to be skulking somewhere about, simply biding his time. Some residue of old memory rose in angry, illogical protest against the whole idea: *He can't hate me that much—not Jess!*

Still he kept a careful lookout as, without a word, he left the group and headed alone at a fast walk across the meadow and into the timber. Damn Jesse. Miss Charley would be waiting at the canyon's end, wondering what had happened, and he was impatient to be reassured that she was all right.

Minutes later, as he broke from the last skirmish line of trees onto the rocky base of the rise, he called out to her. She stepped into sight above and started down to meet him. She had a determined grip on her rifle, but now as they met halfway up the rise, Calem saw that her face was set and pale and the rifle stock was slick with blood.

'You all right, boy? I waited like you said, but I was getting some worried.'

'Never mind about that—you been hit.'

'Shoo, it ain't nothing.'

He took her by the hand and rolled back her blood-soaked sleeve. Her strong pale forearm had been deeply furrowed from wrist to elbow; she would carry an eight-inch scar there, and he only hoped that that was the worst of it. 'Can you move your fingers all right?'

'Shoo, yes. Told you it ain't nothing. An old bullet glanced on a rock and cut it up some. Them fellows was shooting plenty close for a little spell.'

'Cal. Down here . . .'

The well-known voice washed like a breaking wave against his ears; he heard himself say, 'All right, Jess,' before turning his head till Jesse Gault's smiling face touched the edge of his vision.

He stood at the bottom of the rise close to the heavy timber belt which had shielded his silent approach. His fractured wrist, bulkily bandaged, was in a crude belt sling. His other hand was cocked on his hip above his jutting gunbutt. He smiled handsomely, but the effect was gruesome.

'I needed a chance to get you alone, Cal,' he said. 'You got to know who's giving it to you.'

Calem thought, *No, Jess*, as Jesse's hand dipped and came up with a back-hammered pistol. The thought was almost dispassionate; he felt like a man whose muscles had gone to numb jelly on the tail end of a falling nightmare where the ground is slamming up to meet you and you have to wake or die. The feeling was sustained, trancelike, as the shot crashed out, as Jesse heeled over and went down on his face. He braced one hand on the ground, trying in a terrible effort to straighten his arm and roll himself over. He succeeded only in turning his head; then, as his glaring eyes filmed to a gray blank, the arm went limp.

Abel Sutter moved out of the trees like a shadow; he balanced his rifle in the crook of his arm as he bent over the body. Calem came stumbling down the rise, but stopped yards above the place where Jesse had fallen. There was no reason to hurry. His eyes were stinging, and he bit his lip till he tasted blood.

'Figured he was waiting for a chance like this,' Abel Sutter said. 'So was I. I follered you and seen him laid up. I hung back till he made his play.'

'You want me to thank you?'

Old Sutter's eyes gleamed. 'No point, even was you so minded. He killed the best friend a man ever had, but I had no hanker to swing for evenin' the score. I needed me a reason. When he pulled on you, I had it.'

'I sure hope you found it worth it.' Calem's throat felt hot and choking. 'I hope you found it worth all of that horse of yours he killed.'

Sutter eyed the ground for a judicious moment, then spat quietly. 'No, I reckon not. Boy, your brother wa'n't even worth a good hoss.'

*   *   *

In all of his fifty-eight years, Jeffrey Dembrow could not remember speaking words of regret or apology to any man. In a way that single attitude was both the core and the symbol of his iron pride.

He had gone his way too long to change, the Major knew.

Even now.

Strapped firmly down at a supine angle on a pole-and-canvas travois lashed behind his horse, Dembrow let his gaze pass from face to face, as if the answer he sought might lie in one of them.

He was impatient to return to Skull for, among other things, the pleasure of sending his beautiful, murderous daughter-in-law packing back to the saloon from which Ames had taken her, and without a cent to her name. He had never been deceived, as they must all have thought, about Trenna's background, which he had had thoroughly investigated; he had merely wanted to see her mettle fairly tried before passing judgment.

Now he knew. She was not fit to be mistress of the Skull he had built for a wife whom the long years and mellowing memories had left framed in his mind as a prototype of unblemished perfection.

225

Ames—Cody—Trenna. All the young ones, they are all gone. What is there left for Skull—or me?

For a moment the shape of his future, the stark and sterile aloneness of the years that remained, tightened his throat; his lips stirred in a curse and then he pushed the reflection into the safe background of his thoughts.

Almost in a silent cry for reassurance his glance sought the thick, stolid face of Ed Grymes. *It's all right, Ed*, he had said of Ed's frightened lie. No need to tell Grymes that his familiar, thick-headed person was Jeffrey Dembrow's last human anchor, one that, as sorry as it might be, he dared not let go. He needed Grymes close at hand as much as Grymes needed the ancient security of Skull . . .

Jeffrey Dembrow looked at the others, at Duval with his hands tied to his horn and his bandaged throat muffled in a dirty scarf, at Abel Sutter with his stubbled cheek bulging placidly to a working chaw, at the crewmen mounted and watching the Major while they waited for the order to move out.

That time had come, now that he had passed the brutal siege of fever and delirium and was somewhat rested and on the mend. He could delay no longer, and still he could not give the order . . . not yet.

But he could not say the other words either, the ones that he had never said and never would say.

He looked at the two of them standing off a ways. The tall, big-shouldered youth with the gentle, always-brooding eyes of woodsmoke gray, and a shock of black hair lapping down across the high brow of his homely, rugged face. The girl beside him, a head and a half shorter, sturdy as a young pine, the tanned grave pugnosed face livened by the steelbright eyes and crowned by a pale sun-blaze of tangled hair, tomboyish yet somehow more perversely feminine because of it.

If you were a sentimental sort, you would hardly keep from getting a smiling catch in the throat, he supposed, just looking at this ragged and rustic pair who could not be ostensibly, physically, more strangely matched. And yet in those ways that outshone the rags and bumpkin crudeness, so rightly matched. He saw the self-sufficient strength that would bow to nothing, the unflinching and lonely courage that had made do against the bitterest odds he could offer them, and with these things, the splendid and resilient youth that would always hope and fight for a better tomorrow no matter what the odds of now. Jeffrey Dembrow saw, and he knew respect and something else that he had not felt since he was a small boy. And that was shame.

He was seized by an impulse to do something, anything, for these two admirable young people, and the discovery brought a wash of relief; perhaps he could loosely skirt around the other things that would be too hard to say.

'Gault.' His voice had a metallic scratch. 'I want to—I would like to do something for the pair of you. I do not mean as a payment or an amends,' he added quickly. 'It is just something I would like . . .'

His voice slowly trailed as he watched Gault's young face, its expression of reserved neutrality hardening so that there could be no doubt. Dembrow felt chilled.

Gault said in a polite and distant tone, 'Thank you, sir. No.'

'But you have nothing except the clothes on your backs. Surely—'

'Miss Charley's pa left us a good deal of gold. We'll make out fine.' Gault shifted his feet; he tucked his thumbs in his belt, his gray eyes very steady. 'Maybe I should say it plainer. That ain't the reason.' He paused. 'We just don't want anything from you, sir. Not one damned thing.'

Not from the man who had relentlessly hounded him; the flat repudiation stung, but Jeffrey Dembrow could understand. Yet he had failed to pass off what he hated the thought of saying, and his jaw shook with the thought: *I've got to, now.*

'There is one thing you will have to take, young man.' After a heavy pause, he cleared his throat. 'My apology. For making the offer.

For all else that has happened. Will you accept that much?'

Gault hesitated; his head dipped in a brief nod.

The Major leaned his head back; he said, 'All right, Ed, let's get going,' and at Grymes' order, felt the shift of his travois in motion as his horse responded to a tug on its lead rope. The Major wearily closed his eyes to the sudden rattle of hoofs, the creak of leather and the rough lift of men's low voices.

It had not been half hard to say, he decided.

We hope you have enjoyed this Large Print book. Other Chivers Press or G.K. Hall & Co. Large Print books are available at your library or directly from the publishers.

For more information about current and forthcoming titles, please call or write, without obligation, to:

Chivers Press Limited
Windsor Bridge Road
Bath BA2 3AX
England
Tel. (01225) 335336

OR

G.K. Hall & Co.
P.O. Box 159
Thorndike, Maine 04986
USA
Tel. (800) 223-2336

All our Large Print titles are designed for easy reading, and all our books are made to last.